HELD

GONE – BOOK TWO

Stacy Claflin

Receive book updates from Stacy Claflin: sign up here.
http://bit.ly/10NrfMw

NOTE: This book follows Gone, the first book in the trilogy.

Moving

MACY MERCER WOKE up shivering. She rubbed her eyes and then looked around. Once again she was locked inside Chester Woodran's truck bed. Everything was quiet, meaning he was still in the hotel room where he had slept.

At least Chester had allowed her a sleeping bag and pillow, which was a far cry from the last time she had been in there. He had even let her use the bathroom and eat a meal before going to sleep for the night.

It was pretty full back there with everything they had packed for moving to their new home. As usual, she didn't know where they were, or even where they were headed. She actually didn't mind being in the truck bed this time. Not only because of the pillow and sleeping bag, but because she knew Chester wasn't going to kill her. If he had wanted her dead, he would have done it already.

No, he was serious about turning her into his daughter, Heather. Macy was already used to answering to Heather and calling Chester "dad." She felt traitorous to her real dad, but it kept her alive. He would understand.

Also, being in there gave her a break from Chester. He talked nonstop, giving her headaches.

She stretched and sat up. Though it was dark enough in there to not be able to tell whether it was day or night, she could see a little light trying to get inside. This was the day she would see their new home...and meet her new "mom."

What would she be like? Would Macy be given more freedom? The farmhouse had been locked up tight with no neighbors in sight. Would Chester continue to lock her in the new house, or would she have the chance to make friends? She wanted to talk to someone her age more than anything. Well, that wasn't true. What she really wanted was to get back home to her parents and brother, Alex. Then she wanted to run down the street to see her best friend, Zoey.

Macy ran her hands through her hair. It was getting greasy after so long on the road. What had it been? It felt like five days, not that she'd been marking anything on a calendar. It felt like they had been going in circles. She wouldn't put it past Chester to try to confuse her. He didn't want her knowing where they were going.

Not that it mattered since she didn't even know where they had started. She had never been able to figure out where the farm was located. Had they crossed one of the borders and moved into Canada or Mexico? She hadn't seen or heard any Spanish when outside of the truck, so they probably weren't in Mexico, but Canada was a possibility. The times she had been there, it had been pretty much like home.

Would Chester even attempt to cross the border? What if they wanted to search the truck? If they found her, he would be done for. No, he wouldn't do that. He had everything planned down to the last detail, and he wouldn't leave something like that up to chance. Not unless he knew someone who would let him pass, no questions asked.

She grabbed her travel bag and pulled out her last set of clean clothes. She got dressed as fast as she could and then ran a brush through her hair, sure that it didn't do any good. She felt gross and wanted a shower, but she knew better than to complain. She didn't want to find out if the new home had a place for him to lock her up again.

Macy put the brush back into the bag and rolled up her sleeping bag. She sat on it and leaned against some boxes, listening for sounds outside. She heard a car door in the distance, followed by muffled conversation. Chester wouldn't be much longer. He was eager to get to their new home.

Everything was quiet for a while, and then finally, she heard the familiar noise of the lock. She sat up straight, waiting. Was he bringing her breakfast? Most mornings he had. As long as she did what he said, he gave her regular meals and didn't tie her up or hit her.

Bright, morning light assaulted her eyes as he opened the back of the truck.

"You're already dressed? We're going to go into the hotel room so you can take a quick shower—and I do mean quick." He pulled his coat away from his side, letting her see a gun. "Don't try anything funny."

She nodded.

"Don't make eye contact with anyone, and whatever you do, don't talk to anyone."

"Okay."

"Breakfast is already up there. You can eat after you get cleaned up. Then we need to hit the road again. Like I said, today's the big day, Heather."

She climbed out of the truck, carrying the overnight bag. A light covering of snow crunched under her feet. That had to have been why she woke up cold. She looked up to the sky, seeing that it was clear and sunny. She saw pine trees in the distance, reminding her of home—her real home. Her heart ached. Would she ever get to see her family again?

"Come on." He glared at her. "We're not here for sightseeing." He closed and locked the back of the truck, and then led the way to the hotel room. It was a generic, cheap room. He pointed to the bathroom door and then patted his jacket where the gun was.

Going into the bathroom, she let out a sigh of relief at the thought of taking an actual shower. The farmhouse had only had a bathtub, and even though it was stupid to complain about, given everything she'd gone through, she didn't like taking baths. She put her clothes on the counter and stepped into the hot stream of water. The farmhouse water never got very warm, either.

This was like a dream. She knew she was supposed to hurry, but she couldn't help just standing there, enjoying the hot water running down. It almost felt like a massage. She closed her eyes and just enjoyed the experience until Chester pounded on the door and yelled for her to hurry up.

Macy opened her eyes and grabbed the hotel brand shampoo, lathering it through her greasy hair until it felt normal again. Then she spotted conditioner. Conditioner! She hadn't seen that since she had been kidnapped. She took a huge glob and ran it through her hair. She let it sit while she washed up.

Chester pounded on the door again.

"I'm almost done!" Even though she never wanted to get out, she rinsed off and got out. She grabbed the bottle of conditioner to take that with her, just in case. She ran her fingers through her hair, loving how it felt. Once she was dressed again, she put some lip gloss on and took a deep breath before joining Chester.

He was already eating at the little table. She sat down across from him, not making eye contact. A little paper bag sat in front of her. She poured the contents: a plastic fork, a napkin, something wrapped in wax paper and some toast wrapped in plastic fell out. She picked up the mystery item and saw that "vegan" was written on the side.

Was he pleased with her? He wasn't forcing her to eat any animal products? She opened it and saw some kind of breakfast burrito. The smell made her mouth water and she bit down.

"Are you excited, Heather? We get to move into our new home. It's in a nice gated community."

What did gated mean? Macy couldn't shake the feeling that it didn't mean what she envisioned. She nodded, her mouth still full.

"Did you sleep well?"

In the bed of a truck? Macy nodded again.

"Not too talkative, I see. Well, I suppose you're nervous. I would be too, if I didn't know where my new home was going to be. You'll like it. You'll have your own room again. Oh, and you'll finally meet your new mom. I know it's a little soon, but since your mom is off in Paris living the high life with Jacques, we need to move on too. I need a wife and you need a mom. It's not right for a girl your age to be without a mom."

Macy was sure that Heather's mom was nowhere near France, and from what she had read from Heather's diary, Heather hadn't thought her mom was there either. Macy swallowed and kept her eyes on her food.

"Your new mom is so excited to meet you. She's never been married and doesn't have any kids of her own, so she'll be able to devote herself to us fully. She might want to have kids of her own. I'm not sure, since the topic hasn't come up. But isn't this good news?"

Macy's stomach flipped and twisted more than an Olympic diver. "I guess."

Chester nodded. "You're nervous. I get it. Once you meet her, you two will hit it off. Then you'll see how wonderful everything is going to be."

Was the new wife marrying him because she actually *wanted* to be with him? Or was he forcing her to be part of the "family" too? She couldn't imagine anyone choosing to spend time with him, but maybe he had her fooled. He could have put on some hidden charm, pretending to be a great guy. He had probably even used the single dad card to gain her sympathy. Maybe she was one of those people who liked to fix broken people.

Hopefully, this meant things weren't going to get even worse than they already were. Although, her friend Marissa from school had a stepmom—not that Chester's wife would be Macy's stepmom—and she never stopped complaining about her. Every day in Algebra, Marissa had a new complaint about the horrible woman married to her dad.

"We don't have much farther to go today. Would you like to drive in the front with me?"

She looked up at him in surprise.

His light brown eyes peered through the ugly glasses and bore into hers. The corners of his mouth twitched. "I'll even let you pick the music. I can stream any kind you want—no commercials, even."

No commercials also meant no clues as to where they were. Although if she could see signs, that would help. Not that their location mattered all that much anymore. She had given up hope of escaping to get back home to her family. The new house would most likely be as secure as the farmhouse had been. Maybe even more, although she didn't see how. He had mentioned a gated community. Did that mean there was no way out?

"What do you say? We haven't had much time to talk recently, Heather. Dear old Dad has really missed that."

Macy gulped.

"Finish eating that and then give me a hug."

Her heart sank. The only thing worse than acting like his daughter was being locked up in the barn's cellar. Macy ate as slow as possible, wanting to put off the hug as long as she could. He didn't seem to notice. He rattled on about how much she was going to like the new house and her new mom.

He was excited, almost bubbly. Macy noticed that he was sipping coffee. She didn't remember ever seeing him drink it before. Maybe that was why he was in such a good mood.

Finally, she finished her breakfast. There was nothing else she could do to put off giving him a hug.

Chester smiled at her. "Come give your ol' dad a hug, Heather. This is going to be a great day."

Macy's stomach twisted, but she got up and shuffled around the table while he got up from his chair. He opened his arms wide and she pressed herself against him and wrapped her arms around him. He put his around her and squeezed tight, making it hard for her to breathe.

After what felt like an eternity, but was probably only about ten seconds, he let go.

"Let's hit the road. Your mom's waiting."

Exhausted

ZOEY HIT THE snooze button again. Why did her mom insist on her going to school? She could barely function anymore with Macy missing, and going to school did *not* help. The only thing that kept her going was time spent with Alex. They were able to talk, smoke, and…well, keep each other distracted.

If they felt like talking about Macy, they did. If they didn't, they sneaked away somewhere to light up or to one of their bedrooms to forget about everything else. So far, none of their parents suspected their relationship. They just thought the two of them were becoming closer because of Macy's disappearance. Her mom kept saying how Zoey had taken on Alex as her little brother.

The door opened and her mom appeared. "What are you doing still in bed? School's going to start soon."

"I'm too tired."

"You know, they're going to hold you back if you don't keep up."

"They don't hold kids back anymore, Mom. They don't want to hurt anyone's self-esteem. But you know what? At this point, I really don't care. Let them hold me back. I feel like I've been hit by a truck."

Valerie's eyebrows came together and she walked over to Zoey with a look of concern. She felt her forehead and then her cheeks. "You don't feel warm. Do you feel sick?"

Zoey shook her head. "I'm just exhausted, but really, that's not surprising. My life-long best friend has been missing for about a month. What else do you expect?"

She sat down on the bed next to Zoey. "I know, dear. You don't need to remind me. Have you spoken with the counselor at school yet?"

"Ugh. Not that again. I don't need a shrink."

"They're not psychiatrists, and they said a lot of kids have gone in to talk about Macy."

"Yeah, the jerks who feel guilty about bullying her. I have no reason to feel bad—I was always there for her. If I could be, I still would be. No guilt here."

"It's not about guilt. You need someone to talk to, and you sure aren't talking to me about it. Sleeping isn't going to solve anything. The counselor can give you strategies on how to deal with all of this."

Zoey glared at her mom. "I talk to Alex all the time."

"But you need to talk to someone neutral. I'm sure it's good to talk with him since you're both so close to her, but the counselors can offer a different perspective and they've been trained in how to deal with situations such as these."

"Yeah, well, you don't have to go to school and get judged for going to a shrink."

"Why don't I set up an appointment with an outside counselor, then? None of your friends would ever know, although I would question your friendship if they're going to judge you."

"Can't I just go back to sleep? Please. I'm so tired. You have no idea." Zoey yawned.

"What time have you been getting to bed?"

"I went to bed at nine, don't you remember?"

"And you went to sleep then?"

"Yes!"

"If you won't talk to a counselor or go to school today, I'm going to make you a doctor's appointment. Would that be socially acceptable?"

Zoey rolled her eyes. "Fine, whatever. If I can go back to sleep."

"I'll make you an appointment during my lunch break. Think you can be ready by noon?"

She nodded and then re-set her alarm. Zoey closed her eyes and was asleep the moment she hit the pillow.

Traveling

MACY CLIMBED INTO the front of the truck, not allowing herself to get too excited. It was a stupid thing to be excited about, but after having spent days riding around in the back with all of the stuff, she almost couldn't help it.

Chester was still almost giddy, rambling on about a multitude of topics. As she buckled up, he moved aside his jacket, exposing the gun again. Macy stopped breathing for a moment. It startled her to see that, she had almost forgotten about it with his new good mood. Obviously she wasn't supposed to forget it was there.

But he didn't miss a beat. He continued chatting about how great everything was going to be. He couldn't wait to be a complete family again. Once he pulled out onto the road, he asked what kind of music Macy wanted.

It had been so long since he had asked her opinion on anything—actually, he had probably never asked her what she thought about anything. Not since he was pretending to be Jared, anyway. That felt like a lifetime ago and was probably what he wanted. Chester wanted her to feel completely disconnected with her real family.

Macy hesitated. "Is there a top twenty station?"

"Of course. Like I said, I can stream anything." He scanned through the stations until he found one. A song was playing that Macy loved. She and Zoey often sung along to it, sometimes even dancing and using hair brushes or cell phones as microphones. She closed her eyes, welcoming the memories.

Another favorite came on, bringing another flood of memories. This one had been one of Alex's favorites, and there was nothing like watching

Alex dance to a song. He was hilarious and would take up the entire family room, running around and dancing.

Her heart ached. Would they ever get to do that again? When the next song came on, she felt even worse. It was a song she had never heard, reminding her of everything she had missed over the last month.

Macy opened her eyes and saw that they were on a country road. There was nothing except open, grassy fields and livestock as far as the eye could see. She continued to ignore Chester's rambles. He hadn't stopped talking since breakfast.

After about twenty minutes, they drove through a small town. Macy's eyes lit up—she had been there before. She recognized the buildings and even the tiny, rundown park. Her heart beat so loudly she feared Chester would hear it.

A minute later, they were back to being surrounded by fields and farmland again, but her mind wouldn't stop racing. She *had* passed through that town before. It wasn't her imagination. She recognized it. That meant she had been along this road before too. But when?

Macy fought to keep her breathing steady. The last thing she wanted to do was to alert Chester to the fact that anything was amiss. She vaguely remembered being in the car with her family when she had gone through that small town before.

Did that mean they were near her home? Chester probably didn't know she knew where they were. She didn't actually know where they were. Not even the town name signs along the way helped. She had never heard of any of them.

They had to be back in Washington, but where? It could have been on the other side of the mountains or even in the southern part of the state. Or maybe they were in Oregon or Idaho. They had traveled other nearby states plenty of times for camping and sporting events.

Her pulse and breathing finally returned to normal. They went through another half an hour of open fields, only seeing a random grouping of cows or horses every so often.

Eventually, the scenery changed and they were in a forest. The green trees were a nice change of scenery. She was so immersed in their beauty that she forgot to keep paying attention to the road signs. She had always loved that part of the Northwest. Never once had she complained about driving for hours through the woods or mountains.

When they left the trees, they went through another small town. This one had a decent-sized high school and Macy held her breath. There was an actual stop light in this town, and when the stopped, she stared at the school.

She recognized it—and this time she knew why. They had driven there for one Alex's karate tournaments. He had competed in that gymnasium. Zoey had gone with her family, and while they waited for Alex's turn to compete, the three of them wandered around the school and had even chased each other through the parking lot. Alex had been threatening to dump his drink on them.

Where was this town? She really couldn't remember. It had been over a year since they had been there, and she hadn't been paying any attention to where they were back then, either. She thought it was two or three hours from home. The one thing she did know was that it was definitely in Washington.

Even though they were still far from home, they weren't *that* far. Assuming they didn't drive out of state, it was possible she could get away and find her way home. He wasn't taking her to the other end of the country or anything. She couldn't help smiling.

"You like this song, Heather?"

Macy looked over at him. She had almost forgotten he was there. "Yeah, this song is great."

He nodded. "I like it too. It has a good beat." He tapped his fingers on the steering wheel along with the song. Then he moved his left hand down and turned on the blinker.

Where were they going now? The scenery was nondescript; she didn't know how he could tell where he needed to turn. They went down a road to the left that Macy didn't see until they slowed down. It had a gate off to the side, making it look like they were entering private property. There were scrape marks on the pavement indicating that the gate had been opened and closed a lot. Was that what he meant by a gated community?

Her heart picked up speed, but she didn't know why. Wherever they were going couldn't be any worse than the hole in the farm that she had spent too much time in. They were going to a house with a mom…a stepmom. A fake stepmom. Macy twisted a strand of hair.

They drove along the road until it turned into a dirt road. It forked at one point and they went left. Chester finally stopped talking. Was that a good sign? Macy had too many questions, but she had a feeling the answers were coming soon enough.

There was still nothing as far as she could see. Just more grassy fields with the occasional tree.

Eventually, they passed a playground. It looked rusty, like no one had touched it for decades. Chills ran down her spine as she looked at it. She could almost feel the eyes of children's ghosts watching her.

Chester put his hand on her shoulder and she jumped. He didn't appear to notice. "We're almost home, Heather. Are you as excited as me?"

"I…." How was she supposed to answer without lying?

"Oh, I understand. You haven't seen it, so it's hard to be excited. We're almost there."

"Okay."

He picked up speed again. "Just wait until you see it. It'll be different from anywhere else we've ever lived."

That much was obvious. The road became even bumpier. They rode in silence for a few more minutes before he stopped in front of a tiny shack. If that was what it could even be called. It didn't look big enough for more than one room, and there was no way it had any running water or electricity.

"What's this?" Macy asked.

"We need to stop here before we get to the community."

It sound like Macy's blood was pumping right in her ears. She looked around, panicked.

"Is something the matter, Heather?"

She turned to him. "I don't want to go in there." She begged him with her eyes. Maybe if he really did love Heather, he would listen to Macy this one time. "Please."

"Don't worry, Heather. I'll be there with you. I know this building is a little rundown, but it's not our home. It's where we're going to meet some of the residents."

The way he said *residents* didn't sit right with her.

Chester's eyes crinkled as he smiled. "Everything's going to be just fine. You'll see. Let's get out and meet the most important people of the community."

She looked out the windows. What were her chances of getting away?

He patted her shoulder again. "You worry too much. You always have. Just relax."

Relax?

Three men and one woman came out of the building. How had they even managed to fit inside? They were dressed in all white and were headed for the truck. If it was dark, it would have been the perfect setup for a scary movie.

The woman was fairly tall and had her almost-black hair pulled tightly behind her. A man about her height walked with her slightly in front of the other two men. The men all had short hair and the one in front had thick, bushy eyebrows and a beard that looked more like a nine o'clock shadow. The two men in back were taller and thinner, both with dark hair and piercing eyes. They all appeared to be full of confidence, almost like they were on a mission.

Macy clenched her fists.

"It's time to get out." Chester unlocked the child locks and opened his own door. "Come on."

Heart racing faster than ever, she opened her door and got out as slow as possible. She closed the door, but refused to walk toward the people dressed in white.

As they walked her way, their eyes seemed to look into her soul. Their faces showed no emotion, not helping to ease Macy's fear. She wanted to run away, but her feet wouldn't move. These people were probably going to tie her up and leave her somewhere, just as Chester had done when he first took her. She wanted to run—but her body wouldn't cooperate. Fear paralyzed her.

Chester took her hand. Where had he come from? Macy hadn't even noticed him walk around the truck. He pulled on her hand. "We need to meet them, Heather."

Her feet still wouldn't budge.

"Come on. Don't be rude." He pulled on her harder, forcing her to walk or fall down.

Luckily, her feet cooperated. Though she stumbled, she walked with Chester as he held her hand. They stopped when they were only a couple feet from the four creepy strangers.

The shortest man, the one in front, nodded at them. "You must be Heather. Your dad has told us so much about you."

She stared at him, her mouth too dry to reply.

"I'm Jonah and these are my assistants. You'll get to know us quite well. Has your dad told us anything about us?"

Macy shook her head no, hoping that was the right answer.

He smiled, his dark brown eyes squinting as he did. "Good, good. He's followed our directions. Our community is private and we don't discuss it out in the world. Is that something you can agree to also?"

Macy nodded, swallowing. She would be happy never mentioning anything that she had been through, if it meant she had the chance to get away.

"Let's go inside and get acquainted. The sooner we get the rules out of the way, the sooner you two can settle into your home. Your new mom has been busy getting the house ready. She's so excited to meet you."

Community

T HE SHACK WAS nicer on the inside than on the outside. It had a clean, beige carpet that covered the room. Furniture was minimal, but nice. It was all the same color as the carpet. The walls were white and a table with eight chairs sat off to the side.

Jonah pointed to the floor. "Let's sit."

Macy looked at the couch and back to him. Was he serious? All the adults sat down. Apparently he was. She sat next to Chester. It bothered her that she felt more comfortable next to him. But then again, she at least knew that he wasn't going to kill her. The other four—who knew?

No one said anything for a full five minutes. Macy looked around, her pulse still pounding in her ears.

Finally, Jonah looked at her. "Before you two you enter our community, you must go through the purification process to wash the world off. You can't have even a trace."

Macy's eyes widened.

As if answering her thoughts, Jonah continued. "The world is full of evil and we all must become clean before leaving it. Anytime we are forced to go back out there, we must purify ourselves before entering."

Macy nodded even though she had no idea what he was talking about.

"Once you're clean, I will explain everything. Your dad is the head of your household, so he will go first." Jonah rose and so did Chester. They walked to a door that Macy hadn't noticed. Jonah opened it and Chester walked in, closing it behind him.

The lady looked at Macy. "My name is Eve, Heather. I'm looking forward to having you join our community."

"Thanks." Macy couldn't take her eyes off the door the Chester went through.

"Your dad is cleaning the world off."

Just then the sounds of a shower were heard.

Eve continued, "When he has scrubbed its evil away, he will put on clean, white clothes and join us. Then it will be your turn. You'll find the cleaning supplies in the bathroom and it's important that you scrub every inch of yourself. We can't have any remnants entering our land. Will you be able to do that or do you need help?"

"I can scrub myself."

"You'll have to work hard. Your skin should burn."

"Okay. So hard it burns. Got it."

"Good. We'll give you a proper welcome after you've gone through the purification. You understand we can't touch you while the vile world is still on you."

Macy nodded, but had no clue what Eve meant. She had a feeling that she would understand all too well soon enough.

"We'll sit in silence while we wait. Meanwhile, reflect on good and evil."

What did that mean? Macy looked down at her hands, pretending to think about it. It felt like forever before she finally heard the water stop. Did that mean Chester had purified himself? And did that mean she was about to take another shower? Why had he had her take a shower before they left? Did he think she needed to be extra clean?

The door opened and he came out, wearing white pants and a white shirt that resembled a pillowcase with arms and his hair was wet. Beads of sweat broke out around her hairline.

Eve looked at her. She had a serene look on her face. "It's your turn, Heather. Don't touch your dad since he's pure and you still carry the evils of the world."

She had no problem avoiding Chester. Macy got up, never so nervous about a shower. Chester nodded to her, walking far away from her. There was no way a shower had cured him. If they were so worried about keeping evil away, they were bringing it in with welcome arms by accepting him.

She went into the bathroom. It was a tiny room with barely enough room to move around, which was no surprise given the size of the building. Everything was so clean it sparkled. The shower was nothing more than a stall and she saw a pile of white clothes on the counter. Those were her new clothes.

Was she going to have to wear them all the time now? Did everyone in the community wear all white?

Macy noticed a trash can in the corner. She walked to it, seeing Chester's clothes piled inside.

There was a knock on the door. "Do you need help starting the shower?" asked Jonah.

"No. I was just about to start it," she called. There was no lock on the door, so she would have to hurry. The last thing Macy wanted was to have someone walk in on her. She pulled off her clothes and threw them on top of Chester's. The tile was cold on her feet as she walked to the shower stall.

There was only one knob for the shower, and it was market with a "C." She took a deep breath before turning it on. Hopefully it was mismarked and she could still adjust the temperature. Macy turned the knob and gasped as icy-cold water rained down on her. She turned the knob further, finding that it didn't help.

The water was so frigid that it had to come directly from outside, where snow still remained in the shady spots. She had to get out as quickly as possible, but Jonah and Eve would probably check her skin to make sure it was red, showing that she'd scrubbed hard enough.

On the wall hung a scrub-brush and underneath it sat a jug of unmarked liquid that had to be soap. She grabbed the brush, not wanting to think about how many other people had used it before her. She poured some soap onto it and winced. It had a strong, unpleasant odor.

The scent was the least of her problems. The water was still freezing. She didn't have to press very hard for the brush to hurt. Her arm turned red as she washed without adding any extra pressure. She rubbed all over, hoping it would be enough and that they wouldn't send her back for a second shower.

Her teeth chattered in the cold and finally had herself clean for the second time that day. She rinsed herself off and then the brush. Was she supposed to use the soap for her hair? So much for the conditioner she had sneaked in from the hotel. If she used that, they'd know. It didn't smell anything like the soap. She finished the shower and finally turned off the icy water.

Shivering, she found a white towel sitting behind the clothes. She stood for a moment, wrapped in the towel just trying to warm up. What kind of sadists were these people?

A knock started her. "Are you almost done, Heather?" asked Eve.

"Just a minute," she called. Macy toweled off her hair and then put on the white clothes. They were stiff and uncomfortable, but at least they fit. She had been worried that she would have had to wear the same size as Chester.

What was she supposed to do about shoes? Macy looked around and noticed a pair of white shoes sitting against the wall next to the counter. A pair of white socks sat on top of them. At least she wouldn't have to go barefoot.

Macy went out to the main room, her hair soaking the back of the shirt. All five of the adults stood when they saw her. Eve took her hand and brought her to the group. "Now that you've been purified, it's time to go over the rules. Are you ready?"

Holding back a sigh, Macy nodded.

They all sat in a circle. Chester and Eve sat on either side of her. Jonah sat across from her and the other two men sat on either side of him.

Jonah looked Macy in the eyes. "You are indeed blessed, child. Most people never find the true way. It's hidden because of the evil in their hearts and minds. You've been given the gift many never know they want but cannot have."

She continued staring into his eyes. His hazel eyes bore into hers with an intensity she could feel.

"I'm Jonah, as you know, but what you don't know is that I'm the great High Prophet. I receive messages and visions to guide our community in the way of righteousness and pure living. It is my job to take care of my people, seeing to it that everyone makes it to the Holy Land beyond this world. It's my job, for lack of a better word, to find puritans such as yourself: the holy vessels of righteousness who will ascend with me on the great and magnificent day. Do you have any questions?"

Macy shook her head. She did have a bunch of questions, but Jonah wouldn't appreciate any of them.

"You've already met Eve. She's the High Prophetess as my first and primary wife. Eve receives visions also, but not at the volume that I do. Mine are daily, and each evening we gather as a community so I can share what has been bestowed upon me that day with the community."

Awesome.

Jonah indicated to the men next to him. "These are my primary assistant prophets, helping with the community. This is Abraham and Isaac. As you may have guessed from their names, they're father and son."

"Does everyone have Biblical names?" Macy asked. Would she be getting yet another name?

Jonah's eyes narrowed slightly. "Women do not speak to men unless spoken to. I did not ask you just now if you had any questions, but I will let it slide since we haven't yet gotten to the rules. Do you understand?"

Macy nodded, biting back a sarcastic reply.

"I asked you a question. Do you understand?" He sat taller, staring at her with an even deeper intensity.

Eve nudged Macy's knee with her own.

"Yes, I understand."

Jonah's face relaxed. "Good. Now, to answer your question, receiving a Biblical name is a high honor. Only those who have proven themselves get a new name. It's a day of celebration when that happens. We hold a Holy Festival in honor of the occasion. If you're blessed enough, you shall have a festival in your honor. But first, your father must have his own celebration as head of the household. Otherwise, you must wait until you reach maturity."

Macy's head spun. She wanted to put her hands on her head, but didn't dare.

"Now that you have a basic understanding—I wouldn't want to overwhelm you with everything in one day—we'll move onto the rules. You already know never to speak to a male puritan without being spoken to, although some may give you permission to speak freely. That is up to them. As mentioned, every night we gather to hear the message of the day.

Never, ever miss that. It is of the utmost importance. Everyone must hear and apply it to remain pure so we can enter into the Holy Land. We are holy vessels of righteousness, remember."

Using those big religious words must make him feel important, Macy thought.

Jonah went on, explaining things such as proper foods to eat, what constituted as sins, and how the puritans were to cleanse themselves from all unholiness. Basically they had to go through a cleaning like she had just done, or endure a public shaming. Macy didn't ask what that meant.

"Will you be able to remember all of that?" he asked, looking back and forth between Macy and Chester.

Macy shook her head.

Jonah smiled, clasping his hands together. "No? Well, you're being honest. You're truly a chosen vessel, child. I can't express the joy that brings to my heart. Eve will stay in here and drill you on the rules until you have the basic ones memorized. While you two are doing that, I will take the men and we will cleanse, purify, and bless your truck and its contents. Then you may bring them into the community."

Eve took Macy's hand and led her to the couch while the men rose and went outside.

"Can I speak to you without being spoken to?"

"Of course, child. What is it?"

"What are they going to do to the truck?"

"First, Jonah will pray over it as he walks around it. Then the men will lay hands on it while praying and receiving visions. Once all that is complete, Jonah shall anoint it with a special blessing. Afterward, he will wait for a higher vision, and if he gets a positive one, you and your dad will be able to go home."

"That sounds like it could take a while."

Eve nodded. "It gives us enough time to drill you so you know the rules by heart. Are you ready?"

"I guess so."

"You are." Eve smiled. "Do you speak to a brother without being spoken to?"

"Do you mean a man?"

"Any male puritan. Even a child. We do not speak unless spoken to, child. It is the holy way of righteousness. The world looks down on such things, but truly, it is an honor. We are the blessed ones, learning to live in pure submission."

Macy took a deep breath. It was no wonder Chester liked this place.

"When do we go to our daily meetings to learn from the holy visions?" asked Eve.

"Every night."

"Correct."

"Now list for me as many sins as you can recall."

This was going to be one long afternoon.

Unexpecting

Zoey sat in a nondescript waiting room next to her mom. Her mom had her laptop out, working from there. She never passed up an opportunity to get in extra work. Zoey was still exhausted, even though she had slept well over twelve hours.

A nurse opened the door next to the registration desk. "Zoey Carter."

Valerie looked at her. "Want me to go with you?"

"No." Zoey stood up and followed the nurse. She refused to look at the scale, not wanting to know what she weighed. When they got to the exam room, she mindlessly answered basic questions as the nurse typed the answers into a laptop.

The nurse stood and went to the door. "The doctor will be right in. Do you have any questions?"

"Nope." Zoey leaned her head against the wall next to her. She looked at the paper-covered table, wanting to crawl on it and fall asleep. Maybe she would if the doctor took a long time.

Zoey's eyes grew heavier as she waited. Five minutes turned into ten, which turned into fifteen. Finally she couldn't take it any longer, and she closed her eyes. The door opened and Zoey fought her eyes, struggling to open them.

"Zoey Carter?" asked a young, pretty lady in a doctor's coat.

"Yeah."

"I'm Doctor Hernandez. It's nice to meet you. So, you're here for a checkup?"

"I guess."

The doctor sat down and read from the laptop. "You've been over-tired lately? Has there been any stress in your life?"

Zoey laughed bitterly.

Dr. Hernandez raised an eyebrow. "I take that as a yes?"

"You've heard of Macy Mercer, right?"

"The missing girl. Why?"

"My best friend."

A look of sudden understanding washed over her face. "That would certainly explain fatigue. Have you spoken with anyone about how you're feeling?"

"Just my boyfriend."

"No counselors?"

She shook her head. "Just my boyfriend," she repeated.

"You should really consider it."

"That's what my mom says."

"Well, you should listen to her. Anyway, I'll give you a full checkup and make sure that nothing else is going on. Sound good?"

Zoey nodded and then went through another tiring round of questions. Then the doctor looked in her eyes, ears, nose, and mouth, followed by listening to her heart and lungs.

"Everything looks good. One question I have to ask, given your age. I have here that your last menstrual cycle was six weeks ago. Is there any chance you're pregnant?"

Zoey's heart nearly stopped. She stared at the doctor, unable to speak. Was that why she was so tired? Did being pregnant make people tired? Didn't they only throw up in the beginning? It wasn't possible—she couldn't be pregnant.

"Did you hear me, Zoey? Is there a chance you could be pregnant? You mentioned that you have a boyfriend."

She twisted her hands together, unable to find her voice. They hadn't used protection the first few times. The first time had just happened so unexpectedly, and then the next times following were all over the same weekend when she had been staying at the Mercer's house.

"Zoey?"

"Maybe," she whispered. She couldn't be. She just couldn't.

Dr. Hernandez didn't even flinch. She just nodded as though they were talking about the weather. "We have two options. You can either take a blood test and wait for the results or you can urinate in a cup, and then we'll know in several minutes."

"I...I don't know."

She opened a cupboard and pulled out a little cup and then pointed to one of the two doors. "That door leads to a bathroom. Fill this about halfway and then bring back here. A nurse will run the test real quick." She handed Zoey the cup.

"Doesn't the test have to be first thing in the morning or something?" Zoey looked back and forth between the cup and the doctor.

"No. Tests today are sensitive, so it can be any time of the day."

"You're not going to tell my mom, are you?"

"Not unless you want me to."

"No." Zoey grabbed the cup.

She went into the bathroom. Everything felt unreal, but on the bright side, she wasn't tired anymore. The fear got rid of that. How could she be taking a pregnancy test? She was only fifteen—and Alex, he was only thirteen. Sure, he would be fourteen soon, but still.

Her pulse was on fire as she stared at the cup. She barely managed to fill the cup without making a mess. She nearly dropped it into the toilet bowl twice. If she couldn't even pee into a cup, how would she handle a baby?

By the time she made it back to the exam room, her stomach was twisted so tight she could barely breathe. A nurse stood in the room, and she held out a little tray. "Set the cup here, please. Then have a seat."

Zoey placed the cup on the tray, and then sat down. She shook and her mind spun out of control. How could this be happening? Why had they been so stupid? If she would have known they were going to do it, she would have bought protection earlier. She thought for sure they were okay. It was only that one weekend they didn't use any.

Where was that nurse? Or the doctor? Were they trying to teach her a lesson?

Unable to sit still another moment, Zoey got up and paced the small room. What was taking them so long? How long did it take to run a simple test? Didn't they just dip in a stick and get the answer? Were they sitting back there gossiping about her?

Gossip. That's what would happen at school if anyone found out. She wrung her hands together. No. That wasn't going to happen. The test was going to be negative, so she wouldn't have to worry about what people would say.

The door opened behind her. Zoey turned around and tried to read the doctor's face. She couldn't tell either way. Dr. Hernandez had the perfect poker face.

"Why don't we have a seat, Zoey." It wasn't a question.

Zoey sat down, still trying to read her face.

She made eye contact with Zoey. With no emotion she said, "The results were positive."

"What on earth does that mean?" Zoey demanded.

Dr. Hernandez reached over and put her hand on Zoey's. "You're pregnant. The line was quite dark, indicating the probability of a strong early pregnancy."

Everything disappeared around Zoey as she stared into the doctor's dark brown eyes. Her mouth wouldn't budge.

"Do you know what you want to do?" asked the doctor.

Zoey shook her head as tears filled her eyes, blurring her vision.

"There are two options. You can terminate or proceed with the pregnancy. It's your choice, and of course we don't have to tell your parents."

"You'd have to find my dad to tell him—which you're more than welcome to." Anger burned in the pit of her stomach. "That's exactly what he deserves. He's never been here for me and look what happened."

The doctor patted her hand. "Let's focus. You don't have to make a decision today, but if you're undecided, I'll need to send you with some prenatal vitamins. They should help you to feel better, too. The baby is going to continue to take a lot from your body and you really need the vitamins."

"I'll take them."

Dr. Hernandez turned to the laptop and typed for a few moments before she turned back to Zoey. "I'll also send you with some contraceptives."

"It's not like I'm going to get pregnant."

She cracked a smile. "No, but you don't want to get any diseases."

"We're each other's firsts."

"That's what they all say, dear."

Zoey narrowed her eyes. "I've known him forever. He's telling the truth."

"Still, I'm going to give you some. Use them."

Whatever. If she was already pregnant, what was the point? "Fine."

"I'll also get some pamphlets to answer your questions. You'll have some later even if you can't think of any now. There are also some websites listed, you can find more answers there. When you have questions, go to those websites. Don't search online or ask your friends."

"Okay."

"Also, you can call our office anytime, but I'll have the front desk schedule you to come back in four weeks. In the meantime, I'd like you to speak with a counselor. They wouldn't tell your parents anything, either. I can get you a pamphlet for that too. Do you need anything else?"

Zoey's head spun...or was that room? "No."

The doctor typed more into the laptop and then told her a nurse would be in shortly.

Zoey nodded. She couldn't make sense of anything, much less the fact that she was pregnant. The weight of its reality was hitting hard. "How come I haven't thrown up?"

"Not everyone does," said a different voice.

She looked up to see a nurse. Dr. Hernandez was nowhere to be seen. When had they switched places? "Where's the doctor?"

"Oh, she's just talking with your parents."

"Just my mom. My mom!" Zoey stood up. "What's she telling her? I thought she wasn't—"

"She's telling her what she can. Everything except the pregnancy, since you don't want her mentioning that."

"What's there to tell?"

"That you're taking new vitamins and she would like you to see a counselor."

Zoey swore. "I don't want to see a counselor."

The nurse handed her some sample vitamins packs. "These should get you through until your next appointment. You really should decide what to do as soon as possible though. A counselor can help you with that."

She put the vitamins in her backpack. Then she was handed a stack of papers that she probably wouldn't even look at. The nurse spoke, but Zoey couldn't focus.

Home

CHESTER CAME INSIDE with the prophets after what Macy guessed to be an hour and a half of Eve drilling the rules into her head.

Jonah looked at Eve. "The truck and its contents have been purified."

"And the child has a full understanding of the community rules."

"We're all set. Let's show our newest vessels to their home."

Eve rose and Macy followed. They all walked outside and Eve pointed to the truck. "You may travel with your dad."

Macy went into the truck with Chester, and the others climbed into a van—white, of course. Chester started the truck and they followed the van for several miles until they reached a paved parking lot in the middle of nowhere.

After parking, Jonah and company got out of the van and opened the back doors. They pulled out a cart and dragged it to the truck.

Chester looked at her. "You stay in here until we have everything loaded."

"Okay." At least she didn't have to do any heavy lifting. Chester had packed most of their two rooms into the back of the truck.

He got out and Macy could hear the back of the truck open. She bounced up and down in the seat as they removed things from the back. Before long, the back of the truck slammed shut. Chester opened her door and moved aside so she could get out. She slid out without a word.

Jonah looked at her. "We men will pull the cart while you and Eve push from the back. Once we're inside the community, we will have a horse pull it the rest of the way to your home."

Since Jonah hadn't given her permission to speak, Macy went to the back of the cart without replying. The wood was rough and full of splinters. She tried to find a place to push that wouldn't tear her hands apart, but there were no smooth spots. The cart was heavy, and with all of them moving it, Macy still broke out into a sweat before they had even made it a few feet.

It felt like hours, but she really had no idea how long it took to get it to the gate. She wiped her brow when they were done, gasping for air. Her muscles burned.

Eve turned to her. "Before we go in, you and your dad are going to have to wear head coverings."

"Head coverings?"

"You'll need to wear them until tonight's meeting. We'll have your unveiling ceremony to welcome you into the community. Then you will become official members. After that will be the wedding, followed by a time of celebration."

"They're getting married today?" Macy's eyes widened. She didn't even know her future fake stepmom's name.

"Tonight, yes. We can't have you all living in the same house otherwise. She is in another home, getting ready for the ceremonies so that you and your dad can settle in."

The men came around the cart. Isaac carried a pile of white cloth, which he handed to Macy and Chester. Macy held hers up, trying to figure out how she was supposed to wear it. Eve helped her put it over her head. There was only one slit on the head peace, allowing her to see. How was she supposed to breathe?

She looked down and noticed that it hung down away from her shirt, allowing air in.

"One more good push," Jonah called. "We've got the gate open."

Macy groaned. She was already sweating. Wearing the head piece would make it worse.

Eve looked at her. "Hard work is a privilege. It teaches us many things and we should always appreciate it."

"Okay." Macy nodded, unsure if Eve could even tell. They pushed the cart several yards, passing through a thick, wooden gate. Once inside, Jonah and Abraham closed and locked the gate behind them.

The gate was part of a larger fence with no space between the slats. It was about ten feet tall and had metal spikes on the top. No one was getting in or out. The fence went on beyond what Macy could see. As far as she could tell, it wrapped around the entire town—or community, as they called it.

She saw various buildings, some looked like homes and others looked they had other purposes. Macy turned to Eve. "How big is this place?"

"It goes on for miles, Heather. We're entirely self-sustaining with everything we would ever need here inside the walls. It helps to keep the world out. It's unusual for anyone to leave, because there's rarely need. What does the world have that we want?"

Macy could think of several things off the top of her head, but knew better than to say any of them. One of the rules of the community was not to speak of *the world*.

"The horse is attached," Isaac said, walking around the cart. "I'll lead it to the house."

Chester, also covered with head garb, walked with Jonah to the front.

Eve took Macy's hand. "The men will lead the horse and we'll follow behind the cart."

Macy nodded, making sure Eve could tell through the cloth covering Macy's head. Eve let go of her hand and they walked in silence for what felt like more than a mile. The people that they passed, dressed in all white of course, paused to watch them. No one else had anything over their heads.

They were like fish in a tank with everyone staring at them from outside. Macy was glad for the covering, because she didn't want everyone staring at her. She'd never been so embarrassed in all of her life, though she didn't know why. All of the other people were all dressed in the same white clothes as she was, living with the same ridiculous rules she had just learned.

One girl who looked about Macy's age had a large "G" pinned on the front of her shirt.

Eve walked closer to Macy. "That's part of the shaming we discussed. The G is for greed and everyone who sees her knows she committed an act of supreme selfishness. She was already purified, but now must pay the price of her sin."

Chills ran through Macy. What had she done that was so bad? She didn't dare ask, remembering they weren't even to speak of sins committed. They could, however, speak of preventing them before they happened. But they had to be careful, so as not to become tainted.

As they continued to walk, more people came out of homes and buildings to watch the newcomers. What were they hoping to see? The only thing they could see was how tall they were and maybe their eyes, but no one came close enough to get a good look.

Macy tried to tell what she could of the people, but they were mostly nondescript, all wearing the same white clothes. The girls and women had their hair pulled back in tight buns, some of them wearing odd, white hats. The guys all had super short hair, and again, some wore hats, while others didn't.

Finally, they stopped. The horse and cart stopped first, and then Macy and Eve stopped also. She looked around, seeing a few small homes on either side of the dirt road. They all looked the same. Which one was going to be their new home? Not that it mattered. Wherever they moved wasn't going to be her *home*.

Jonah walked to the house closest to their left. He opened the door, not appearing to have unlocked it. Were there no locks?

Seemingly out of nowhere, about a dozen men showed up. They removed items from the cart and carried them into the house.

Eve took Macy's hand again and tugged. They stepped back several feet.

"We'll let the men do the heavy lifting. Once everything is inside, you two can settle in. Remember to keep the covering on until it's removed in the ceremony. Then and only then can it come off."

Chills ran down her spine. "Why doesn't anyone have a coat?"

"We don't wear coats. Suffering and trials lead us on the path to purity."

"What about when it snows?"

"No coats. Some go out in it specifically to become more pure. Sometimes it can turn into a fun competition." She smiled, her eyes shining.

Yeah, that sounds like a great time, Macy thought sarcastically.

Before she knew it, she and Chester were inside the chilly, little house, unpacking. She got the shivers again. "Is there no heat?"

"You're not to speak until spoken to, Heather."

Macy's stomach dropped. She stepped back. Was he going to hit her? Lock her up? Make her wear a letter?

"You're free to speak—don't worry." It sounded like he was smiling behind his curtain of white. He actually sounded joyful. "Just don't forget it when other males from the community are around. About the heat: electricity is believed to be one of the evils of the world. See that wood stove?"

"Yeah." She looked at the small, black stove in the corner.

"I'm told those keep the homes nice and toasty. Would you like me to start a fire?"

"Yes, please. I'm freezing."

"Have a seat and make yourself comfortable."

Macy stared at him. Was he serious? He wasn't going to put her to work? She sat on the couch, pulling a heavy afghan over herself.

"Your new mom made that. She made a lot of things in here."

"Have you even met her?" Macy asked.

Chester picked up a log from next to the stove and shoved it in. "Yes, although not in person yet. We've been corresponding through letters. She's excited to meet us."

Macy looked around the room, feeling like she'd stepped back in time. Everything looked like the *Little House on the Prairie.* A few years before, she and her mom watched all the seasons. Macy never would have guessed the show would become her life one day.

Chester looked at her through his head dress. "It might take a bit for this to warm the place up. Why don't you unpack your room and get settled in? That way you don't have to worry about it after the wedding."

"Uh, sure." She rose, keeping the blanket around her.

"I'll get the rest of our stuff ready."

She found her bedroom. It was a tiny room with just a bed, a shelf, a desk, and small dresser. Obviously, they didn't have a wide variety of clothes, so a large dresser or a closet was unnecessary.

Macy set a box on the bed and opened it. She gasped. Her teddy bear was on top. It was the one that she had had at home—her real home—

that Chester had stolen and teased her with. How long would she have it back? Picking it up, she smelled it. It mostly smelled like the farmhouse, but when she breathed deeply, she could smell her home.

Images of her room filled her mind. She heard a noise outside the room and stuffed the bear next to the pillow. Could she find a place to hide it so that Chester couldn't take it away again?

Disagree

AS SOON AS school was out, Alex texted Zoey again. She hadn't texted him all day, and he needed to know what was wrong or if everything was okay. He had texted and called a bunch of times during lunch, but her phone had to have been off because it kept going to voice mail.

He found an empty seat on the bus and sat by himself, hoping everyone would leave him alone. He was tired of all the questions about Macy. As if it wasn't bad enough that he had to deal with his sister's disappearance, he also had to put up with everyone's stupid questions and comments.

He sent another text, and just as he hit send, someone sat next to him. He groaned, not caring if he hurt anyone's feelings.

One of the jocks looked at Alex. "Hey, dude. Any news on your sister?"

Alex jumped up. "You really think if there was, I'd just be sitting on the bus?"

"Whatever." The jock shrugged and went to the back.

Alex looked out the window, ignoring everyone else until he reached his stop. The house was empty. His dad had had to go back to work not long after Macy disappeared, and his mom often went out look for Macy or passing out fliers.

After eating a banana, he threw his bag into his room and headed back outside. If Zoey wouldn't answer his texts, he'd go to her house.

When he got to her house, only two houses away, Valerie answered.

"Sorry to bother you, Ms. Carter. I didn't know you were home." Maybe that was why Zoey was ignoring him.

"You're never a bother, Alex. I'm just working from home today.

Zoey hasn't been feeling well and I wanted to keep an eye on her."

"Is she okay?" He regretted the urgency in his voice, but he couldn't help it.

"I think all the stress of the last month has finally caught up with her. You should take care of yourself too. The doctor gave her some vitamins to help with her energy. You might want to look into getting some if you're tired."

He was already on anti-depressants, but he wasn't going to tell her that. He hadn't even mentioned it to Zoey. She probably wouldn't care, but it was still embarrassing. "I'll keep that in mind, thanks. Can I talk to her?"

"I think so. She's locked herself in her room. Want me to check on her?"

Zoey appeared around the corner behind her mom. "I'm up. Can I walk around the neighborhood with Alex? I bet some exercise and fresh air will do me some good. Right, Mom?"

Valerie looked relieved. "I'm so glad you want to get out of the house." She gave Zoey a hug and then tousled Alex's hair. "I love that you two are still close, even with Macy missing. How are your parents, Alex?"

He shrugged. "Still getting along, but upset about Macy. Sometimes I hear them crying when they think I'm not listening. It sucks."

"I wish I could do something to make this better. I'm worried sick about Macy. If anything ever happened to my Zo, I don't—"

"Mom, please don't." Zoey pushed her way around Valerie and stood next to Alex. "We won't go far, okay?"

Valerie nodded, still giving him a look of pity. "Do you guys have someone making you dinner? I haven't heard from homeowners' association. They were the ones putting that list together.

Zoey grabbed Alex's arm. "Mom, if they need you to make dinner, they'll ask."

Alex nodded. "After everyone from the HOA made our meals, some church took over. I think there are even some other churches that want to help too. We're covered for a while, but thanks."

Valerie leaned against the door frame. "Oh, good. Okay, you two have a good walk. Be home by dinner, Zo."

"Okay." Zoey managed to give that one word three syllables. She yanked Alex down the driveway. "Can you believe her? I swear, she never knows when to stop talking."

He shrugged, pushing some of his bangs out of his eyes. "She's not so bad. Did you turn your phone off? I texted you, like, a million times."

"I slept all morning and then I forgot my phone at home on the charger."

"You should at least check it, you know. I was worried something had happened."

"Sorry." She looked like she meant it. "I just haven't been feeling myself lately. I need more sleep or something."

"Is that what the doctor said?"

"Something like that." She looked up at the dark clouds. "It's going to snow again. I hope Macy's somewhere warm."

Alex's heart sunk. "I hope so too. But she's smart. She can take care of herself."

"Not smart enough to come home."

Alex scowled. "It's okay to admit it hurts. You don't have to say crap like that."

Zoey rolled her eyes. "Did your shrink tell you that?"

He pulled his arm from her hold. "What's with you?"

Her eyebrows came together. "I'm. Tired."

"No, it's something more than that. What's going on? Tell me."

"Nothing," she said, way too fast.

"Whatever. Don't tell me. I'm only your boyfriend who loves you." He walked faster, forcing her to speed up if she wanted to catch him.

"Alex, come on."

He stopped and turned around, letting her catch up. He grabbed her arm, forcing her to stop too. "You're keeping something from me. Why? Just tell me something so I'm not completely in the dark."

She yanked her arm away. "I'm just under a lot of stress. I'd think you'd understand that."

"Don't give me that. If you don't want to tell me what's bothering you, just say so."

"Fine. I don't want to talk about it." She crossed her arms and stared at him.

"At least you're finally admitting it. Let's go smoke. I really need one after today."

A strange look came over her face. "I'm going to skip that today."

"Really? Why?"

"Because. Got a problem with that?" Her eyes were shining. Was she about to cry?

Alex felt bad, but at the same time it irritated him that he didn't know what was going on. What was she keeping from him?

"I've been thinking about cutting back, Alex. Let's just keep walking."

They walked through the neighborhood, not saying anything. Alex tried to think of what he would have done to make her so mad.

Irritation continued to build in his chest until he couldn't take it any longer. "If you have something you don't want to tell me, that's fine. Just don't take it out on me. If I did do something to you, just tell me. I deserve that much."

Sounding bitter, she laughed. "It's not like that. Look, I have some things I need to figure out. Once I've got my thoughts organized, I'll let you know."

"Does it have anything to do with me?"

"You're not going to give up, are you?"

"Nope."

"Maybe I should just go back home."

"Maybe you should." He stared at her.

"Alex, please don't do this."

"Don't do what, exactly?"

"This."

"Congratulations. We're having our first fight. Call me when you're ready to make up." He spun around and headed back home, more frustrated than before. He would have been better off not even going to her house. Ever since Macy disappeared, they had stuck together, telling each other everything. Why was she pulling away now?

He walked fast, muttering to himself, not knowing if Zoey was following him or not. Part of him wanted her to be so they could talk about whatever was eating her, but part of him also hoped she had turned around and went home the other way. He didn't need her to take her crap out on him. He had the rest of the world for that.

Hopefully, whatever was going on with Zoey was temporary. But what if Macy's disappearance was too much for her now? Could she be ready to move on with her life? What if she wanted to get rid of every reminder of her best friend, including him? He stopped and leaned against a tree.

Zoey wouldn't want that, would she?

A minute later Zoey walked in front of him and stopped. "I didn't think you'd ever stop." She sounded out of breath.

Alex narrowed his eyes. "Are you going to break up with me? If so, just tell me."

"What?" She looked genuinely shocked. That was a good sign.

He frowned, not showing her his relief. "You heard me."

"Break up with you? Why would I do that?"

"How would I know? You won't tell me what's going on."

"So you jump right to me dumping you?" Her lips formed a straight line.

"No. It took forty minutes of walking and thinking to come to that. Best I can figure—since you won't tell me anything—is you don't want to hurt anymore, so you're moving on with your life. Getting rid of all the Mercers from your life."

"Why would I do that?"

"So you don't have to deal with the pain of Macy being gone. I'm just a reminder of her."

She looked at him like he was crazy.

"It sounded better in my head." He looked away.

"Oh, Alex." She wrapped her arms around him. "The last thing I want is you out of my life. I don't know what I'd do without you. Besides, I know Macy's coming back. Sure, it's been like a month, but she'll be back. If she doesn't, she knows I'll beat the crap out of her."

Alex breathed in the sweet smell of her silky, jet-black hair. It smelled fruity. "I'm glad to hear that. The part about not dumping me."

"You'd have to try a lot harder than that to get rid of me."

Dinner

MACY MOVED THE curtain a little and peeked outside. It was starting to get dark already, but that wasn't surprising, given that it was December. But what did surprise her was how many people were outside, wearing only their white garb. Did they wear any layers underneath?

At first, it appeared that no one was paying attention to their house, but as she looked closer, she noticed eyes turning their way, scanning the home. Were they as curious about her and Chester as she was about them? No one was staring hard enough to see her curtain barely moved out of the way.

She could hear Chester calling her from the other end of the house. Macy found him in the kitchen.

He looked her way, still wearing the head piece. "The ceremony will be soon, Heather. We should eat something."

Macy was glad they would remove the headpieces soon. It was challenging only looking through a slit. "Where's the fridge?"

"There's no electricity here, remember. See that? It's an icebox, and it holds the same purpose."

"How are we going to cook anything?" she asked.

"On the wood stove, of course. It looks like your mom made us some stew. Can you grab a pot from over there?"

She nodded and went to a metal rack that held pots and pans. She picked one that looked about the right size and then turned to Chester. He closed the icebox and held a ceramic bowl in his hand.

"Set that on top of the icebox and I'll pour in enough for us to eat. We shouldn't waste any, because I don't know yet what to do with leftover food. Clearly there's no garbage disposal around here."

Macy almost said something about not wanting to wear a "W" for wasteful, but thought better of it. He was in a good mood and she didn't want to do anything to disrupt that. She held the pot still while he poured the stew. Even though she had the fabric over her face, she could smell the meat.

As if reading her thoughts, Chester said, "I know it's not vegan, but at least it's organic. They don't use any kind of chemicals or hormones inside the community walls. Everything is exactly as nature intended."

Macy didn't care about the meat. She'd eaten enough since Chester took her that she wasn't a vegan anymore. Maybe someday, if she ever got away from him, she could be one again.

He pulled the bowl away and put the top back on. "Would you put that on the stove, and then come back to find a wooden spoon? I'm going to see what else we can eat."

She nodded, almost unsure how to respond to him being so nice. Why wasn't he barking orders? His politeness was unnerving, but the last thing she was going to do was to question it. She carried the pot to the wood stove. She hadn't realized how much room it had on top, but it had plenty of room for cooking meals.

Macy went back to the kitchen and explored the drawers until she found a wooden spoon. She went back to the living room and stirred the stew, which was already starting to bubble. Her mouth watered; whatever spices had been used smelled delicious.

When it was warm enough, she brought it back to the kitchen where the table was set for two. A fruit salad and a loaf of unsliced bread sat in the middle of the table. Chester's back was to her at the counter.

He turned around. "That was fast."

She sat down and then he joined her. Once her plate was full, she realized a problem. "How are we supposed to eat with these things covering our heads? We're not supposed to take them off, right?"

"We'll have to lift them. Just be careful not to get anything on it."

"Okay." She pulled it out and then up, but it covered her eyes. She was able to see down, but just barely enough to see her plate. "Can we just take them off to eat? It would be a lot easier, plus we wouldn't get them dirty."

"No. We have to follow the rules, Heather. Just be careful." He sounded the tiniest bit irritated.

"Okay. I was just asking." Macy held onto the covering with her left hand while feeding herself with the right. It took some maneuvering, but she managed.

When her plate was empty, she still wanted more, but she didn't want to deal with eating any more while holding the fabric. "What do we do with the dishes?"

"Wash them in the sink, of course."

"But there's no electricity."

"It's pumped in from a well outside. It's not warm, but it's clean. It's a lot better than the chemical-filled crap in the city."

"Don't you mean the *world*?" Macy covered her mouth, afraid he'd get mad at her for making fun of the community.

He laughed. "You're right. It's not like what they have out in the world. I think you've been paying more attention than me. We ought to hurry. The ceremony will start soon."

Macy took that as her cue to get up. Her mouth watered for more stew, but she ignored her hunger. She had to use both arms to pump the water into the sink. Chester had been right. The water looked clearer than she was used to.

She put her hand in and jumped back. It was ice cold—it was even worse than the shower she had taken earlier.

Chester laughed again. "We can warm it in a few of the pots. I'll help you in a minute, Heather."

Macy filled a pot with water, put it on the stove, and then went back for another. Before long, the water was the right temperature and she had a sink full of warm water. She mixed in some soap. It was had the same horrible smell that she had been forced to use in the shower earlier.

She heard Chester put something in the icebox and then he stood next to her, drying off the dishes she had just washed. He chatted about the house, telling her that they would warm their baths the same way, and then he explained the clothes would be washed in some kind of a basin.

He continued to talk until they had the kitchen clean. "Let's sit in front of the fire, shall we?"

"Okay." Macy followed him to the couch as he carried an oil lamp. It did an okay job of lighting up the rooms, but it didn't compare to a light bulb.

Chester sat down and Macy sat at the other end of the couch, as far away from him as she could get. He scooted closer until he was right next to her. Then he put an arm around her. "Aren't you excited about becoming a family again, Heather? We're going to have a mom, dad, and child. It's a beautiful thing. Who knows? We may even have more children. In fact, we probably will. I can't imagine they allow birth control here." He laughed again.

Macy squirmed. She didn't want to talk about birth control or him making babies with his new wife. Time to change the subject. "What's her name?"

"You'll call her Mom, but her name is Rebekah."

"Is that her real name?"

"It's her new name. Like us, she came from the world, but she ascended into her role in the community. That's why she's now allowed to get married."

"Even though you haven't ascended?"

"Correct. Jonah received a vision about me rising in the ranks quickly. I'm going to be the fastest person to become a prophet. I'll need to prove myself, but then our family will be one of the revered ones."

"How did you find the community if they never leave?"

There was a knock on the door.

Chester gave her a hug and then opened the door. A freezing cold gust blew in. Macy hadn't realized how well the little stove had warmed the house up.

Jonah and Eve stepped inside. Jonah looked at Macy. "Are you ready for your unveiling, Heather?"

"Yes," said Macy, since she had been spoken to directly.

"Good. Once we've completed that ceremony, we'll have the wedding. Then you get to come home as a family. This is a truly blessed day."

Eve walked over and took her hand, helping her off the couch. "Everyone is so excited to meet you two. Jonah has had so many visions and messages about your dad. I'm sure you already know what an amazing man he is, worthy of the reverence to be bestowed upon him."

All eyes were on her, so she nodded.

Eve let go of her hand and then took Jonah's.

Jonah raised his other hand. "Let us go. The time has arrived."

Ceremony

MACY TOOK IN the large room. She'd never seen so many people dressed in all white before. A hushed whisper ran through the room as people turned to look at them. There wasn't much to see. Their heads were still covered. They probably looked creepy—at least Macy thought so. Everyone else looked at them, appearing to be in awe.

They had another thing coming if they expected Chester to be a great prophet. He would only be able to keep his facade for so long before his true colors showed.

Jonah raised a hand and the crowd moved aside, creating a path. Jonah and Eve walked down first, hand in hand. Chester took Macy's hand and they followed. Macy was aware of all the eyes on her.

Once they reached the front of the room, Jonah let go of Eve's hand and raised both of his hands. All at once, everyone in the crowd sat on the floor. Jonah motioned for Chester and Macy to move to the left. Abraham, Isaac, and some lady stood at their right. Was that one of their wives, or was it Rebekah?

Stepping forward, Jonah looked at the crowd. "Tonight is a most special night. Not only do we have an unveiling and a wedding, but we are unveiling a future prophet. I've been sharing my visions of him since before his identity was revealed. He is the person who will rise to become a prophet faster than anyone besides myself. This is a most exciting night, is it not?"

"It is." The group spoke as one.

Jonah walked back and forth. The room was so quiet the only sounds were of his shoes moving across the floor. The anticipation could be felt. Macy knew it wasn't just her nerves, but everyone before her was eager to see their future leader.

"I have received yet another vision this very afternoon." Jonah stopped and scanned the audience again. "It has been solidified and confirmed. The man here before you," he pointed to Chester, "is going to become a prophet even sooner than we believed. In three months, he shall be your newest prophet."

Gasps ran throughout the crowd.

"I know," Jonah replied, his eyes wide. "He is chosen specifically from above. There is a mission for him to complete, though what it is has yet to be revealed. I think he will help lead us into the great and mighty Promised Land, but that is purely conjecture on my part." He paced back and forth again.

Eve walked up to him. She carried two red flowers.

Jonah looked at her. "You may speak."

She faced the crowd. "The time has arrived for the unveiling." She handed Jonah the flowers. Together they walked over to Chester and Macy.

Macy swallowed, nervous. As she looked at all the people watching her, beads of sweat formed around her hairline.

Jonah handed Chester one of the flowers, and Macy the other. He turned around and touched Chester's arm.

Chester let go of Macy's hand, which she had forgotten he was holding. Her heart picked up speed.

Placing his hand on the top of Chester's head covering, Jonah looked back to the crowd. "And now I give you Chester Woodran." In one quick movement, he pulled the fabric off Chester's face.

Everyone rose and bowed. "Chester Woodran." It sounded more like a chant than actual speaking.

Jonah raised his hand and everyone sat.

"And now I give you his daughter—your new sister. Heather Woodran." Jonah walked around to the other side of her and yanked her head piece off. Macy could feel her hair pull up with the covering. Her hair had to have been sticking out in every direction.

The crowd stood again and gave a less dramatic bow. "Heather Woodran." Then they all sat.

Eve walked over to Macy and pulled her hair back into a tight bun. She then whispered in Macy's ear, "You must always wear your hair like this outside of your home."

Jonah paced again. He spoke of more visions and messages that he had received that day. Macy tried to pay attention. She didn't know if she would be quizzed. But she felt too self-conscious, standing in front of so many people.

Jonah turned to face Macy. It felt as though he was reading her thoughts. Somehow just having him look into her eyes made her feel exposed. Eve took her hand and led her to the middle of the stage, where Chester met them.

Waving his hands, Jonah came to stand with them. He spoke in words that Macy had never heard before. It sounded like another language, although it was nothing like one she had ever heard before. He raised his hands up high and Abraham and Isaac walked over.

Jonah placed a hand on top of Macy's head. She looked over to see he had his other hand on Chester. He was speaking faster and Macy still couldn't understand a word.

Her instincts were to run, but she knew better than that. Even if she could get out of the building, there was no way of escaping through the fence. Then what? Chester would be mad at her for ruining the ceremony. He would lock her up for sure.

Something wet fell on her head and dripped down the sides, running through her hair. She looked up to see Isaac pouring something from a small jar over her. Abraham had a similar bottle and poured yellow liquid on Chester, although he didn't have as much hair to catch it.

Once the bottles were put away, Jonah turned to the crowd again. "They have now been anointed with oil and are officially part of our great family. Now it's time for Rebekah to come up so we can have the wedding."

Macy looked through the audience, anxious to see the woman she would soon be calling "Mom." She couldn't see anyone at first, but then at the far end of the room, someone rose and walked over. She wore the same white clothing as everyone else. Didn't she want to have a special dress for her wedding day?

As she came closer, it was obvious that Rebekah was young—not all that much older than Macy—and beautiful. Even with her hair pulled back tight, no makeup, and wearing a nondescript white outfit, her beauty shone. If she lived outside the community walls, she could easily be a model or an actress.

She finally made it to them and she stood near Jonah and Chester.

Jonah looked over the crowd. "Now we are about to have a new family unit. Nothing is more prized than family. We are all truly blessed this day, but especially these three."

Macy couldn't take her eyes off Rebekah. She looked over and they made eye contact. Rebekah smiled, easing Macy's nerves.

Rebekah walked to the other side of Chester. Jonah still spoke about the importance of families. Macy couldn't concentrate.

It might not have been so unnerving had she been away from people for so long. For the last month, she had only been with Chester and his parents. She'd spent a lot of time alone, especially when he had her locked away under the barn.

Jonah raised his voice, startling her. He practically shouted about the beauty of marriage. He said it was an everlasting, eternal gift that would follow them into the beloved Promised Land. He lowered his voice and looked into the eyes of Rebekah and then Chester.

The silence made Macy's ears ring. Jonah knew how to make his voice take up the entire building, and when it stopped, deafening silence followed.

"And now," boomed Jonah, "I pronounce you husband and wife. Let the festivities begin."

Everyone stood, clapping.

Chester took Rebekah's hand and they both bowed.

No kiss? Even though Macy wasn't excited about the wedding, if it could even be called one, she felt gypped with no kiss.

Macy turned to Eve, who was still close. "No kiss?"

Eve shook her head. "Public displays of affection aren't appropriate. Are you excited? Now you have complete family unit."

Before Macy could respond, Jonah shouted again. "Time for a grand celebration. Eat, be merry, and meet our newest brother and sister."

"I need to help bring out the food." Eve squeezed Macy's hand and walked off, followed by Abraham and Isaac.

Macy stood, watching the scene before her. People were lined up in front of Chester and Rebekah. Everyone was speaking, the noise making Macy dizzy. She wanted to run.

Jonah put his hand on her shoulder. "Stand by your parents and greet your new brothers and sisters. Everyone is excited to meet you."

Macy made her way to Chester, standing at his side. The lady speaking with him turned to her and clasped Macy's hands into hers. "It's so wonderful to have you two join the community. We've been looking forward to your arrival. Personally, I can't wait to see your dad grow into his role and become anointed as a prophet." Her eyes lit up and she squeezed Macy's hands. "We'll have to have you over for dinner soon. Oh, I'm so excited." She grinned and then walked away, allowing the next person to gush over Macy and Chester.

By the time the last people in line finally walked away, Macy was exhausted. Everyone was eating. Somehow while they had been meeting everyone, the room had been transformed into a banquet hall. Chester smiled, looking back and forth between her and Rebekah. "Shall we join them and get something to eat?"

Rebekah nodded. "Yes. I'd like to officially meet Heather first, if that's okay, Sir."

Sir?

Chester stood taller, obviously enjoying it. "Of course. I should have introduced you myself. Heather, this your new mom. Rebekah, this is Heather."

Rebekah smiled wide, showing perfectly straight teeth. She had to have come from *the world* also, because no one was born with teeth like that. She gave Macy a hug. "It's such an honor to meet you. You're so beautiful, Heather. You look just like your dad. Do you hear that all the time?"

Before Macy could respond, Isaac and Abraham walked up to them. Isaac looked at Chester. "You three will join us at our table tonight. Follow us."

Chester took Rebekah's hand and then Macy's. Chester and Rebekah marched forward with smiles on their faces. Macy fell behind a little, and Chester tugged on her hand. Macy picked up her pace to walk in line with the two of them.

They made their way to the table, finding plates already waiting for them. Chester sat first, followed by Rebekah. Macy sat at the end, next to Rebekah.

Macy wasn't particularly hungry because of her nerves, but she ate anyway.

Decisions

Z OEY STARED AT her Geometry book, unable to concentrate. How did anyone expect her to get anything done? Was life just supposed to carry on like her best friend *hadn't* disappeared without a trace?

Was she supposed to go to counseling and that would solve everything? Right.

Zoey's eyes became heavy again. How long would she be so tired? Every time she sat down, she wanted to sleep. The last thing she cared about were isosceles triangles, so she climbed into bed. She would at least be only a year ahead of Alex if she was held back.

She closed her eyes, but instead of sleep all she could see was Alex's hurt expression when they were arguing. He knew she was hiding something.

Obviously she'd have to tell him about her doctor's appointment. More than that, about their baby growing inside of her, making her so tired. It didn't even feel real—how could she have a *baby* in her stomach?

Aside from being exhausted, she didn't feel any different. Did she look different? Zoey got up and stood in front of the mirror. She had bags under her dark brown eyes, but otherwise looked exactly the same.

She pulled off her shirt and examined her stomach. It was still flat...but for how long?

One thing she knew was that she wasn't getting an abortion. Over the summer, she had taken her friend Tara to get one and it almost killed her. Tara had begged Zoey to go with. She hadn't told anyone else, including the guy. They lied so Zoey could be in there during the operation and said that they were sisters, even though it was pretty obvious they weren't. Tara had bright red hair and Zoey was half-Japanese, thanks to her absent dad.

Everything had been going well with the procedure, as they kept calling it. Then Tara's face lost all of its color and her eyes looked cloudy. Zoey had been sure that Tara was going to die in front of her.

The nurses shoved Zoey out of the room. She was left to worry in the waiting for what felt like an eternity. She hadn't been able to get the look in Tara's eyes out of her mind. Every time someone came into the waiting room, she expected them to tell her that Tara hadn't made it.

Tara ended up being sent to the emergency room at the hospital. Zoey had to take the bus home alone, worried about Tara. She had to act normal when she got home, but it had taken months for the image of Tara to stop haunting her dreams. In fact, it was Macy's disappearance that distracted her.

She hadn't even been able to talk with Tara after the ordeal. Her family moved before school started and all of her social media accounts had been deactivated. Tara's parents had probably figured out what happened and freaked out, moving her away from all the bad influences. Like there wouldn't be other kids just like their group of friends wherever they moved.

Zoey's mom walked in, bringing her back to the present.

"What are you doing? Oh, Zoey, you've lost weight. You better take those vitamins the doctor gave you. I don't want to see you waste away, dear."

She almost laughed. Losing weight was the least of her concerns. "I'll be fine. I just haven't been hungry lately." She put her shirt back on.

"Are you hungry? The Mercers invited us over for dinner. Alyssa said they have enough to feed ten people."

Could she face Alex's family? Zoey could barely even look Alex in the eye, how would she face Chad and Alyssa? They would probably hate her when she had to come clean. The news people watched every little thing they did. Sometimes there was even a van out in front of their house, recording. She might destroy their reputation.

There had been a few times that Alex hadn't been able to sneak out to see her because of the stupid van. The last thing they needed was for his sneaking out to be broadcast to a popular online page.

"Zoey? Are you listening?"

"Sorry." Zoey shook her head, trying to clear it. "Yeah, let's eat at their house."

"Maybe that'll pull you out of your funk. Why don't you brush your hair?"

"Whatever."

Before long, they were over at the Mercer's eating from a huge spread. Dishes were piled high with food across the table and there was even more on the counters. A large pork roast sat in the middle of the table surrounded by mashed potatoes, a green bean casserole, fruit salad, a pasta dish, and even more.

"Is this supposed to last all week?" Zoey asked.

"You'd think," Chad said. "But it's just tonight's meal. I think that church is trying to fatten us up."

Alex wasn't saying much. Zoey could tell he wanted to know what she was keeping from him.

How would he react? He was only thirteen. He wouldn't want to become a dad. There was no way.

What if he got mad at her? Her stomach twisted in tight knots. She kept her eyes on her plate and forced herself to eat. As good as everything looked and smelled, she couldn't bring herself to eat much.

"Are you okay, Zoey?" Alyssa asked. She looked concerned.

"Just not too hungry today."

"I know what you mean. My appetite has fluctuated a lot over the last month."

She nodded, pretty sure that Alyssa's eating habits were due to Macy being gone, and not from being pregnant. Although she and Chad had been getting along lately. It was still doubtful.

Looking around, Zoey's appetite decreased even more. What would everyone around the table think of her when they knew? The Mercers had been her second family for as long as she could remember. Would they tell her she could never see Alex again? The sleepovers would definitely stop.

Her mom would find someone else for her to stay with when she went on business trips. Maybe she would even stop taking them altogether. Or maybe she would finally hunt down Zoey's dad and make him get involved in her life. That wouldn't be so bad. Zoey could think of some choice words to throw at him.

Somehow she made it through dinner, barely eating anything, yet pretending to eat more than she had. After she and her mom cleaned up the kitchen, she found Alex in his room.

He looked up in surprise. "Come on in." He patted the bed next to him.

She sat down, noticing that Alex didn't scoot closer.

"Do you want to sneak out later for smokes?" he asked.

She shook her head.

"You're serious about cutting back?"

"I've been having too many lately. I'm gonna get hooked if I'm not careful."

He raised an eyebrow. "I thought you already were."

"Whatever."

"Want to make out?"

"You could just kiss me instead of talking about it. It would be more romantic that way."

"Yeah, but you've been acting weird today. I don't want to do anything to upset you."

She sighed, too tired to argue.

"What's going on? You know can tell me anything."

"Not this." She shook her head.

"Why not?"

Tears filled her eyes, and Alex's face softened. He pulled her into a hug and held onto her, not saying anything. He really was a good person, she knew that. That was why she had hooked up with him in the first place. Most boys her age were jerks, or at the very least, idiots. He actually cared and he was smart and sweet.

Maybe she should just tell him. They'd been talking about everything for so long, and she hated keeping anything from him.

"Alex, I'm pregnant."

Silence.

She turned to look at him and he was staring straight ahead, his face pale. He dropped his arms from her sides.

"Alex?"

He looked at her. "You're… you're… p…pregnant?"

"That's what the doctor said."

His eyes grew increasingly wide. "Did they give you a test?"

She nodded. "It was a strong yes, apparently."

Alex jumped up and punched his dresser. He let out a string of profanities and then looked at Zoey. "What are we going to do?"

"You don't have to do anything. I—"

"Of course I do. I did this to you, Zoey." He picked up a book and chucked it across the room.

"Well, the thing is, I'm not getting rid of it." She explained what happened with Tara. When she got to the part about her nearly dying, Zoey cried so hard she shook. "I'd never been so scared of anything in my life. I never even got to talk with her after, because her parents wouldn't let her talk to any of her friends before moving her away."

Alex sat down next to her. "That doesn't usually happen. I mean, if it did, no one would get abortions. I heard about a girl getting one at my school last month. She's fine. She's on the tennis team and she didn't stop playing or anything."

Zoey shook her head. "After seeing Tara like that, I can't. I don't know if it's that post-traumatic stress thing or what, but there's no way. I'd rather get fat for a few months."

"But it's nine months. That's practically a year. Zoey, come on. You don't wanna do this to yourself."

"I don't care. It's better than dying."

"You won't die. I'll go with you and hold your hand the whole time. I swear I'll—"

"No." Zoey moved away from him.

Alex was quiet for a minute. "Are you gonna tell your mom?"

"I guess when I can't hide it any longer. She's gonna be pissed, but it's not like she can do anything about it."

"We should tell our parents together."

"No. I'm going to leave you out of it. Just let me take the fall. You're family's dealing with enough."

"I can't let you do that. It's not fair. You didn't do this to yourself. It was me."

"Look out front," Zoey said. "There's almost always a news truck out there. Everything you guys do is broadcast to the world. Do you want *this* all over the news?"

Alex balled up his fists. "Still, I couldn't live with myself if I let you deal with all alone."

"Just pretend to be a good friend, standing by my side. Besides, then we can keep our sleepovers."

"I'm not that kind of guy. I can't do that to you."

"No one needs to know who the dad is."

Alex looked like he was going to be sick. "I can't believe you just called me a dad."

"That's what you are. Sorry."

"You really won't consider an abortion?"

Zoey glared at him. "Didn't you hear a word I said?"

"Just checking. What about adoption? Then we won't be parents. Someone else will be."

"I'm going to keep it, Alex."

"You've really thought this over." Alex frowned.

"After seeing what happened to Tara, yeah. I've gone over this a million times, wondering what I would do if I got pregnant."

"But you don't have to *keep* it, keep it. We can pick out a nice family."

"No."

Alex took a deep breath. "Then we really need tell our parents."

Zoey shook her head. Maybe he really was too young to handle this, because telling their parents was not the answer. It wasn't like they spilled flour—she was pregnant. "Not yet. I need some time to figure this out."

"What's to figure out? You said you're keeping it." Alex narrowed his eyes.

"I don't know what I want to do! Okay? Are you happy?"

"Happy? Of course not."

They stared at each other.

"I never should've told you," Zoey said.

"What? Yes, you should have."

"Now we're fighting—again. This is going end up ripping us apart."
Angry tears filled her eyes.

Alex's face softened. "Nothing's going to keep us apart." He kissed her
cheek. "I'm not leaving your side, Zoey."

"Thanks." Zoey examined his face. He looked genuine, but could she
really trust him? Would he really stick it out, or would he walk away like
her dad had? Only time would tell.

They sat in silence before Alex finally spoke up. "We don't have to tell
them today, but we have to soon. It's not going to take long for you to
show since you're so skinny, you know?"

She leaned against him and sighed. "I know."

Family

MACY WAS RELIEVED to see her teddy bear still sat on the bed where she had left it. She took off the stiff, white clothes and put on her favorite pair of Heather's pajamas. They felt luxurious after the cardboard-like white clothes.

She took out the hair tie and shook her hair free before blowing out the candle. She made her way into the bed. It was stiff, just like the clothes. The blankets weren't particularly soft, either. Apparently, fabric softener wasn't something they used in the community.

Squeezing the bear tight, Macy closed her eyes. Even though the bed wasn't comfortable, it was better than being in a sleeping bag in the back of the truck.

Just as she was starting to drift off, a squeaking noise startled her. Her first thought was mice, especially after having been in the barn cellar. But it wasn't that kind of squeaking. It was a rhythmic, ongoing sound.

There was a thud, followed by silence. Whatever it was appeared to stop. Macy rolled over, closing her eyes again, relieved to finally be going to sleep.

After a few moments of quiet, the squeaking began again. Squeak, squeak, squeak. Squeak, squeak, thud. Squeak, squeak, squeak. Squeak, squeak, thud.

What *was* that?

She closed her eyes tighter, knowing that wouldn't help as the sounds continued. Was that something she was going to have to get used to sleeping through? Was it some kind of non-electrical machinery from somewhere in the community?

The rhythm was interrupted by another noise. What was that one?

Macy sat up, clutching the bear. It sounded like a moan. A moan? What would…?

Oh, no.

Squeak, squeak, squeak. Thud, moan. Moan. Squeak, squeak, squeak.

No, no, no. It was Chester and Rebekah's wedding night.

Squeak, squeak, squeak.

"Gross, gross, gross." Macy threw herself down and covered her head with the pillow. She could still hear the noises despite having the pillow over her head.

She let go of the bear and pushed her hands over the top of the pillow. But she could still hear it and now that she knew what it was, it was even worse than before. That was the last thing she wanted to listen to, and it made her stomach sick.

"Make it stop," she begged to any force that might be listening. "Please."

Where were her earphones when she needed them? She would have to make her own music. Macy picked one of the songs she had heard on the radio on the way to the community and hummed the melody, focusing on it.

After she was done with the song, she listened for the noises.

Squeak, squeak—

Macy pulled the pillow back over her head. Were they ever going to stop? She hummed another song and managed to fall asleep.

When the early light of the morning shone on her face, she woke up. Macy rolled over, hoping to get more sleep. Instead, her mind raced.

Would they give her a job or would she be allowed to go to school? Macy couldn't imagine Chester letting her out of his sight, even within the impenetrable walls surrounding the community.

Would she be allowed to make friends? She had met some teens the night before. Maybe some of them were nice. What if one of them wanted to escape also? They could work together to find a way of escape. She'd have to feel everyone out, which meant acting like she was happy to be there.

She was becoming a first class actress, having learned how to pretend she was Heather, and that Chester was her dad. All she would have to do was to keep up that performance, adding in a fake belief in the prophets. Then if there was someone like her, Macy would be able to find them and get them to open up to her.

Acting like Heather had gotten Chester to be nice. It could probably gain even more benefits with a full community of people.

Though she hadn't spoken a word of her family in what felt like a lifetime, she made sure to keep them in the forefront of her mind. She often thought of her parents and Alex, constantly calling her parents Mom and Dad in her mind. There was no way she was going to let go and give into Chester.

Calling him Dad and *believing* he was her dad were two separate matters. She had to cling to her family, and so far, she had done a good job of it. They were alive and well in her mind.

There was a knock on the door.

Maybe they would leave her alone if she pretended to sleep. She stuffed her bear under the covers and closed her eyes.

Another knock. She held perfectly still, forcing herself to breathe naturally.

She heard the door open and footsteps head toward her.

"Heather?" It was Rebekah.

Her stomach turned. She didn't want to look at either one of them after last night.

"Wake up, Heather."

Macy held still.

"Heather, it's time for breakfast. I don't know what you like, and I want to make something you will."

Macy rolled over, rubbing her eyes. "Is it morning already?"

Rebekah smiled. She was wearing the white clothes everyone wore, but her hair was down and she was even prettier. Macy wondered what she would look like with a little makeup. Probably gorgeous.

"Do you like eggs?"

Obviously Chester hadn't told her about Macy being vegan. Her stomach rumbled.

"Is that a yes?" Rebekah smiled again, showing off her perfectly straight teeth.

"Sure."

"Oh good. Today we get to take it easy because your dad and I got married last night. We don't have to go to work or school."

Macy nodded. "Okay."

"Take a few minutes to wake up, and then come out for something to eat. I'm looking forward to getting to know you." Rebekah left the room, closing the door behind her.

She sat up and stretched, smelling food. Her stomach growled again.

Would it be okay for her to go into the rest of the house wearing the green pajamas? Rebekah hadn't put her hair up, so maybe it was okay to be lax.

She had to go to the bathroom, which was nothing more than an outhouse in the back yard. Macy would definitely have to wear white to go out there because the fences between houses were so low that if anyone was in their own yard, they would see her.

Smelling the breakfast, she decided to wait. She was hungrier than anything else. Besides, wearing her pajamas in the kitchen would be a good way to test what she could get away with inside the house.

A noise outside her room startled Macy. "Is she up?" asked Chester.

Rebekah said something, but it was too muffled for Macy to understand. "I'm up!" she called.

"Hurry up, Heather. It's time for breakfast."

Macy made her bed, knowing that having even the slightest mess in her room sent Chester over the edge. She held the bear from home, whispered *I love you* to her parents and brother, and then looked around for a good hiding spot. If she pissed him off, Macy didn't want him hiding the bear again.

There weren't many spots, but she had brought some of Heather's stuffed animals. Maybe if she put the bear with those, he wouldn't be able to tell the difference between that one and the others. She could hope. That was all she had.

She opened her door. Chester stood looking at her. He was wearing his white clothes.

He stared at her pajamas. "In the future, you're to get dressed in appropriate clothes before leaving your room. Technically, we shouldn't even let you sleep in those, but I suppose no one else will know. Just like how you have your hair down."

Macy looked at the pajamas. They had a high collar and covered her from ankles to neck. How were they inappropriate? Because they weren't white and uncomfortable?

She nodded.

Chester put his hand on her shoulder. "Let's see what Mom has made."

Macy held back a cringe. How was she going to get used to calling Rebekah *Mom?* Not only was she not her mom, but she was so young, barely older than Macy.

They went to the living room which was toasty warm from the fireplace. "I told Heather that she can wear these pajamas for now, but after today, she has to put on her white clothes before coming out here."

Rebekah turned around and smiled at Macy. "I don't mind her wearing those. They look comfortable." She looked at Chester. "But if you don't want her wearing them, it's your call."

Macy wanted to throw up. She was going along with his head of the household crap, too.

"Are you ready to eat?" Rebekah asked her.

"Yeah."

Chester squeezed her shoulder, but not too hard. "No informal speech in the community, Heather."

She looked at him, confused. What had she said wrong?

"No 'yeah' or other slang. A simple yes will do."

"Don't feel bad," Rebekah said. "It takes a while to get used to living here after being in the world. I still slip up once in a while, and I've received my true name. Grab a plate from the kitchen. It's almost done."

Arguing

ALYSSA PUT THE ferret back in its newly clean cage. She hated cleaning it, but she wanted it to be nice when Macy got back. Macy loved the little guy, and even Alyssa couldn't deny how cute he was. The irony was that she had been close to threatening to get rid of it because Macy hadn't been cleaning the cage. Now here Alyssa was cleaning it herself without complaint.

Ducky ran around, checking out every inch of the multi-level cage. Alyssa sat on the bed, watching. After a few minutes, she looked around the room and noticed that it was getting dusty. Macy couldn't come back to a room full of dust. Alyssa grabbed a clean rag from the pile of cleaning supplies on the floor and got to work.

When she was about halfway through the room, she heard the door creak open. She turned around to see Alex watching her. He looked pale and scared.

Alyssa's stomach tightened. "Is everything okay? Is there news about M—?"

"No, but I need to talk to you."

She had never seen him so worked up before. "Sure, honey." She set the rag down. "Have a seat."

"No, I mean with Dad too. He's in the living room."

"This doesn't sound good."

Alex didn't say anything.

"Let's go." They walked in silence downstairs, Alyssa's mind racing with possibilities. When they got to the living room, Chad was sitting on the couch, but he wasn't alone. Zoey and Valerie were sitting on the two recliners.

Her heart picked up speed. She looked at Chad. "What's going on?"

"That's what I'd like to know," Valerie said. "No one will tell me anything."

Alex and Zoey looked at each other, and then Alex sat on the love seat with her. Alyssa sat next to Chad.

"Why are we here?" Alyssa stared at Alex.

Zoey took a deep breath and sucked her lips inside of her mouth. A nervous habit Alyssa had seen since Zoey was little. Alex took Zoey's hand and Alyssa looked at Valerie.

Alex sat taller. "We have something to tell you guys. Please hear us out, and don't start yelling."

"I don't like the sound of this," Alyssa muttered.

Chad took her hand. "Just tell us what's going on."

"We want you to keep an open mind, Dad."

Alyssa could feel Chad tense up next to her. "It's getting less open the longer you stall."

"I'm pregnant," Zoey said.

"Oh, honey," Alyssa said. "I'm so sorry."

The look of shock on Valerie's face was crushing.

"Who's the fath...?" Alyssa's gaze wandered to Alex and Zoey's intertwined hands. "Alex?"

Alex nodded and then put his arm around Zoey. "We're in love."

"No." Alyssa covered her face. "No, you're not."

Chad sat up straight. "Is this true, Alex?"

He looked at the ground and nodded. "What were you thinking? Didn't you use protection?"

Alex narrowed his eyes. "You never even gave me the sex talk, Dad."

"Don't blame this on me!" Chad stood up. "Talk or no talk, you've had health classes. We signed the waivers for you to sit in on those discussions."

"How could you do this?" Alyssa asked, her eyes filling with tears. "Alex, you're just a baby yourself."

Alex's eyebrows came together. "Obviously I'm not, Mom."

Alyssa looked at Zoey. "And you!"

Zoey's eyes widened. She scooted closer to Alex.

"We invited you into our home and cared for you like a daughter—this is how you repay us? By taking advantage of our son? He's only thirteen. Thirteen!"

Valerie stood up. "She hardly took advantage of him. I'm pretty sure that he knew exactly what he was doing. Zoey didn't force him to ejaculate into her."

"Mom!"

Chad stood between Valerie and Alyssa. "Maybe we ought to sleep on this and discuss it when we're not all in shock."

Alyssa stood up. "I don't see what that'll accomplish. It's not going to change anything." She looked at Zoey. "I know you could have had an abortion without telling your mom. Are you planning on keeping the baby?"

"I'm not having the procedure."

"So, you're going to raise a baby at sixteen? I suppose you're going to want Alex to pay child support."

"What? No."

"Of course he will," Valerie said, stepping forward. "He did this to her."

"Okay, okay," Chad said. "What we all need is a break. We're too upset to discuss this right now."

Alyssa glared at him. "What does that have to do with anything? We don't need to be calm—it's not going to change anything."

Valerie moved around Chad and stared at both of them. "How could you two allow this to happen? I trusted you to take care of my daughter. Not only did she run into an intruder here at your house, but Alex and Zoey slept together right under your noses."

"Oh?" Alyssa narrowed her eyes. "Like it couldn't have happened at your house? If you were so worried about it, why did you even have her stay here in the first place?"

"I thought she was safe!"

Alyssa took a couple steps closer to Valerie. "She never once got hurt, not even when someone broke in."

"Hurt? What would you call this?"

"Look, Valerie, you've left her over here plenty of times over the years.

She's been spending the night since preschool, and you've always known we have a boy here. It hasn't been a secret."

"Yeah, but I didn't think you would let *this* happen."

"Let it happen?" Alyssa clenched her fists. "What exactly were we supposed to do? Stay awake all night to make sure they both stayed in their own rooms?"

Chad stepped between them again. "Clearly, no one saw this coming—"

"Except your son!"

"And your daughter." Alyssa raised her fists. "Stop talking about Alex like he's some kind of monster. He's only thirteen. You think he would turn down the advances of a girl so much older than him? He's the—"

"Oh, would you stop with the 'he's only thirteen' crap, Alyssa? He knew exactly what he was doing to Zoey."

Alex stood up. "Stop! Would all of you just stop?"

Everyone stared at him.

"Zoey and I have been in love for a long time now. Like, way before Macy even disappeared. We didn't tell anyone, not even Macy. We saw each other right under all of your noses and no one thought anything of it, of us spending so much time together. I'm not sure why. I guess because nobody thought I was good enough for Zoey. But she thinks so, and you know what? I love her. She wanted to keep me out of this and not tell anyone it was me. But you know what? I told her I wouldn't do that to her. We love each other and you guys better get used to it."

Alyssa's mouth dropped open.

"You—" Valerie started.

"And that's not all," Alex continued. "Yeah, we made a mistake the first time we did it. We should have used protection, but it just happened. We were so stressed about Macy being gone and we weren't thinking."

Valerie glared at him. "I hope you enjoyed it, because you aren't going near her again."

Zoey got up from her chair and grabbed Alex's hand. "That's where you're wrong, Mom. We didn't tell you to get your permission to keep seeing each other. We told you to let you know what's going on. We could have dealt with this all by ourselves, but since I'm not having an abortion, we thought you needed to know."

Alyssa sat back down on the couch. "Where did I go wrong?"

Zoey looked at her. "I'm really sorry about this, Mr. and Mrs. Mercer. Really. You guys are already overwhelmed with everything about Macy. I know because it's killing me too. And Alex." She held up his hand. "I don't want you guys having to worry about the news finding out about this. I won't tell anyone else that he's the one."

"You think they won't figure it out, Zoey? They park across the street and have seen you come into our house countless times."

"But that doesn't mean they'll figure it out. I'm Macy's best friend; they'll probably think I have a boyfriend somewhere else."

Chad shook his head. "Alyssa's right. We appreciate you trying to protect us, but even if it was another boy, they would still speculate."

Valerie's eyebrows came together. "She's trying to protect you guys, but who's protecting her?"

"Mom, would you shut up?"

Fury covered Valerie's face and she slapped Zoey across the face.

Zoey's mouth dropped open. She put her hands on her face. "Mom!"

Alex jumped toward Valerie, but Chad blocked him. "Like I said, we all need to calm down before we discuss this. We're only going to say or do something we regret later."

"What's there to discuss?" Valerie yelled. "We're never speaking to any of you ever again. Come on, Zoey, we're leaving."

"I'm not going anywhere. You hit me!"

"That wasn't a hit. You're so dramatic. That's your problem: you think everything's worse than it is. It was a slap, and you're not injured. We're leaving."

"No."

"No?" Valerie asked.

"You heard me. I'm staying here. At least you don't have to worry about me getting pregnant."

Valerie gasped. "How dare you? I was never worried about that from the start—not here." She glared at Alex. "We need to go home and talk about getting that procedure done."

"I already told you: I'm not getting it done. I could have done it without you ever knowing, so you definitely can't force me. If you're worried about what everyone is going to think, you're going to have to get over it."

"We'll talk about it later. Come on."

"I'm not going anywhere."

Valerie looked at Chad and Alyssa. "If you let her stay here, I'm reporting you for kidnapping."

"Kidnapping?" Alyssa exclaimed. "Have you lost your mind?"

"If you do that, Mom, I'll report you for hitting me."

"You wouldn't."

Zoey narrowed her eyes. "Watch me."

Alex put his arms around Zoey. "Can't you guys just calm down? We need you guys to support us more than anything."

Valerie turned to him, raising her hand. "Support? You want support, you little—"

Chad stepped in front of her again. "Put your hand down, or you really will have problems, Valerie. You don't want to lay a hand on anyone else. Understand?"

"Don't tell me what to do, Chad. You have no idea what my life is like."

"I do know there are laws, and you have no right to lay a hand on anyone."

"Zoey isn't staying here. This is the last place I will ever leave her again."

Chad looked at Zoey. "If you ever feel unsafe for any reason, you can come here." He turned to Valerie. "We know you're a good mom and you don't want to hit anyone. We're all under stress now, and I have no idea what's going to happen tomorrow, but Alex is right about one thing. We need to pull together. We've always been friends. Heck, we've taken vacations together. Remember?"

Valerie took a few steps back, looking deflated.

Alyssa took Chad's hand and looked at Valerie. "He's right. We need to be here for both kids."

Valerie's lips formed a straight line and she sat down.

"Can we agree to sleep on this?" Chad asked. "There's really no way we're going to be able to have a reasonable conversation now. We need to calm down and process everything. All of us."

"Fine," Valerie said. "But I'm not allowing my daughter to spend the night in the same house as Alex. If Zoey wants to stay here, then Alex comes home with me."

Alyssa and Chad exchanged a look.

"What do you think?" Chad asked her.

It was a crazy idea, but she wasn't about to say anything to set Valerie off further. "I can live with that." Alyssa turned to Alex and Zoey. "Kids?"

Zoey folded her arms. "I'm not going anywhere after she hit me."

Valerie's eyes narrowed. "It was only a slap, Zoey."

"I'm not going anywhere."

Alex stood up. "I'll go over there."

Zoey jumped up and glared at Alex. "I can't let you do that. I'll go home."

"Aren't you afraid I'll hurt you?" Valerie asked, her voice dripping with sarcasm.

"Not with a police cruiser across the street."

Valerie shook her head.

"Let's get back together tomorrow," Chad said, "and we can talk with clear heads."

"All right." Valerie stood up. "I have evening meetings at work, but I can get away at lunch."

"Lunch it is," said Alyssa.

"I can't wait," Zoey mumbled.

Phone

ALYSSA FLIPPED THROUGH the channels, unable to sleep. She kept thinking about going back to that bar the next town over and drinking herself stupid again. It had been nice to escape from the pain and stress, even if it had only been for a short time and it was pathetic to get drunk alone.

What if Rusty, the tow truck driver, wasn't there again? If it hadn't been for him, Alyssa wouldn't have gotten home that night. That wasn't entirely true. She could've called a cab, but then she would have had to explain to Chad why her car was at a bar.

She needed a drink more now than she had before. How could Alex have gotten Zoey pregnant? Right under their noses, no less. Was it because she hadn't been paying enough attention to him? She and Chad had been so focused on Macy's disappearance that they hadn't been giving him the focus he deserved.

They hadn't even taken him to a single karate practice. He probably felt like he didn't matter; that all they cared about was Macy. The poor kid was lonely and desperate for attention and if he and Zoey were already developing feelings for each other, then Alyssa had given him the perfect setup.

Tears filled her eyes. This also was her fault. If she had kept a better eye on Macy, she wouldn't have been able to sneak out. And if she hadn't been so focused on Macy, then Alex wouldn't have thought he had to turn to Zoey. The hot, angry tears spilled down her cheeks. All of this was her fault. Her family was falling apart and she could have prevented it all.

Alyssa put the remote down, ignoring a dog food commercial. She looked around the family room, filled with so many memories. The kids had taken first steps in here. Macy pretended to be a rock star countless times, singing along with her favorite songs. Alex practiced for his karate tournaments in here. They'd had countless movie and game nights. They'd had friends over, birthday parties, family gatherings, and the list went on.

Alyssa swallowed a sob, not wanting to wake anyone. Chad and Alex had finally fallen asleep not that long ago. The three of them had spent hours talking, mostly listening to Alex. They had let him talk about anything and everything, wanting to make him feel like the most important person in their lives. They knew, too late, that they needed to give him more attention than ever before—not less, like they had been.

He told them how much he missed his sister and how he wanted to punch half of the kids at school for making stupid comments. Alyssa had started to tell him that violence wasn't the answer, but when Chad reminded her that they were there to listen, she stopped talking. Alex went on to talk about how much he adored Zoey. At first, he seemed to be testing the waters, to see how they would respond. When Alyssa and Chad listened without judging, he had really opened up.

It warmed her heart to see Alex opening up to them like that. She wished that it hadn't taken Zoey getting pregnant for that to happen. She wanted more closeness with him. Alyssa had always adored him, but had forgotten because of her grief over Macy.

Something caught her attention on the news and she turned to look. She thought she had heard Macy's name. Not that it should have come as a surprise. Despite there being no new clues, she was still a story each night locally. The national stations had moved on, at least somewhat. They still brought her up once in a while.

Alyssa had heard wrong. The news wasn't discussing her daughter, but instead showing a fire. The building looked familiar. It took her a moment to realize it was their dentist office. She realized everyone had missed their appointments a few weeks earlier.

One of Macy's pictures from one of her online accounts appeared on the screen. In the image, Macy was talking on her new phone. It looked like a candid; probably one that Zoey or another friend had taken.

Macy's picture shrunk and moved to the top right of the screen. A reporter held a microphone to some guy holding something. Alyssa squinted to see what it was. It looked like a broken phone.

Her heart dropped to her stomach when she made the connection. Had someone found Macy's phone—smashed? She tried to pay attention to what they were saying on the TV, but she couldn't process the words.

She pulled her own phone out of her pocket and scrolled, looking for the police department.

"Detective Fleshman."

"What's going on, Detective? Did someone find Macy's phone? The news, they—"

"Mrs. Mercer?"

"Yes, yes. What's going on with my daughter's phone? Is that what they're talking about? Is it true?"

"We just got word. Some idiot looking for his fifteen minutes of fame went to the news instead of us with evidence. Officers Anderson and Reynolds just left to take care of the situation. You might want to prepare to come down to the station, Ma'am. Once we have it in our possession, we'll likely need you or your husband to identify it."

Alyssa dug her nails into the coffee table. "So, it really could be hers?"

"We have no way of knowing until we have it. But at the same time, it could just be some attention seeker with a similar phone."

"Am I supposed to just wait until I hear from you guys?"

"That's about all you can do."

"I can't just sit around, waiting. Can we go down there and look at it when it arrives?"

"We have to process it first."

"Process it? What does that mean?"

"It means paperwork. I know our job looks glamorous—" Fleshman chuckled, "—but a lot of our time is spent filling out forms."

"Can you call me before you start the paperwork? That way we can at least get down there a little sooner."

"Will do, Ma'am."

The call ended and Alyssa threw her phone on the couch. If it really was Macy's phone, did it mean anything? When they found her bloody clothes, nothing had ever come from that. They were her clothes and the blood was hers, but it hadn't led to her.

It felt like an eternity had passed since then. The world was still moving along as though nothing was wrong. Alyssa's entire life was upside down, and now with Alex's news, even more so. How was she supposed to deal with her daughter being missing *and* her little boy becoming a father? It didn't even feel real. Alex was just a kid himself.

Not long ago, his voice had been cracking. He didn't even have braces yet! Alyssa put her face in her hands. What had she ever done to deserve all of this?

Sighing, she looked back up at the TV. They were still discussing the phone that appeared to be Macy's. How long until the police got the phone and called her?

She leaned back, watching and listening. It didn't sound as though they really knew anything useful. The phone was missing the battery—she and Chad knew that. They had gotten Alex and Macy the most expensive phones available to keep the kids safe. A lot of good that had done.

They would need to bring Alex's phone to the station. If the smashed up phone was in good enough shape, Alex's battery would bring it to life. They would know right away if it was her phone. She had a picture of herself with the ferret as the screen saver. Even if they couldn't get past her password, that alone would tell them it was her phone.

What if they couldn't get the battery in? How would they know it was her phone or not? The guy who found it could have been lying. What if he just wanted to get on the news?

Didn't she have the boxes the phones came in? The company had told them to hang onto those because they had serial numbers or something. She jumped up from the couch and ran to her room, straight for the closet. She dug around, looking for the boxes. She couldn't remember where she had put them.

Alyssa made a mess of their walk-in closet, but she didn't care. She had to find the boxes.

"What's going on?"

She jumped and turned around. Chad stood just outside the closet, rubbing his eyes.

"Someone found a phone that looks like Macy's. I'm trying to find the box, so we have the serial number."

"I put those in the garage."

"What? Why?" She stood up, bumping her head on a shelf.

"So they wouldn't get lost. I know right where they are. Did the police call? I didn't hear it ring."

Alyssa shook her head, picking up some of the things she had thrown on the floor. "I saw it on the news. Some guy found a phone that looks just like hers, but instead of taking it to the cops, went straight to the news."

Chad rolled his eyes. "Of course. Are we supposed to go down to the station?"

"Not yet. They don't have the phone, but as soon as they do, we can go."

"Why can't they ever find evidence at lunch time? Let me get some pants on and I'll get the phone boxes."

"Sure." Alyssa put the rest of the stuff away. She had nothing else to do while she waited for Fleshman's call anyway. His call—wait, her phone was in the family room. She dropped the slipper in her hand and ran to the other room. No new calls.

She heard the garage door slam shut downstairs. Chad must have found the box. Now it was a matter of waiting—again. They were always waiting for something.

Learning

"**H**EATHER?"

Macy mumbled something not even she understood. It couldn't be time to get up already—she was too tired. She'd had to hum herself to sleep again after spending the day learning from Rebekah how to run the household, which was now their job to share.

"It's time to get ready for school," Rebekah said.

"Why so early?" Macy stretched and opened her eyes. The room was dark, although she could see a little bit of light from behind the curtain.

Rebekah held a candle. "It starts soon and we need to get breakfast ready. You're going to help me."

"Can I have a shower—I mean a bath? I feel disgusting. Oh, sorry. That's not very...what was the word Ch—" Macy coughed to cover up her mistake. "—Dad used? Formal?"

"It's all right. I'm not going to get you in trouble for informal speech. I want to help you adjust to living here in the community. It's a lot to take in after living out there."

She reached over and brushed some hair out of Macy's face. Something on her arm caught her attention. "What's that?" Macy asked.

Rebekah pulled her sleeve down closer to her wrist. "It's a mark of shame from my old life."

"A mark of shame?"

"Let me speak plainly for a moment. I was in a pretty successful indie band. We lived the wild, dream life most kids in the world aspire to. Our songs had thousands of downloads, our videos had even more views, and our shows were always packed. My tattoo was a mark of pride, and is now my shame. I keep it hidden and now only your dad knows about it."

Macy's eyes grew wide. Rebekah was not only beautiful, but cool. "Can I see it?"

The corners of Rebekah's lips twitched as she obviously tried to hide a smile. "Promise not to tell anyone?"

"Yeah. I would pinky swear, but I'm sure you don't do that."

"This one time won't hurt anything." Rebekah held out her pinky. She smiled.

Macy couldn't believe it. Maybe she'd actually have a friend. In her house, even. Sure, Ingrid and George had been nice, but they were like grandparents, not a friend. Her eyes lit up and she slipped her pinky around Rebekah's.

Rebekah's eyes twinkled. "Remember, a pinky promise is for keeps."

"Of course. I can't wait to see it."

Rebekah pulled up her white sleeve, exposing a black and white sun with several symbols in the middle.

"What is it?"

"It was the logo for our band."

"That's awesome. I wonder why I've never seen it if you guys were so popular."

"We were mostly known on the east coast, where I'm from."

"Why did you quit?"

"To join the community."

Macy's mouth dropped. "For real? Why?"

"I was chosen."

"How? Why did you—?"

Rebekah pulled her sleeve back down. "I'll tell you everything, but later. We have to get ready for school. You'll need to get dressed and pull your hair back. I can help you with that if you need me to."

"No bath?"

"Sorry. We usually only bathe once a week unless we need to be cleansed."

"Feeling gross isn't enough?"

She put her hand on Macy's. "Your body will adjust and you'll stop feeling that way soon. All of the shampoos and soaps from the world strip away our body's oils, making us produce unnaturally high amounts. In a way, this is another way of purifying ourselves from our time out there."

Macy sighed. "I'll be out in a minute."

Rebekah squeezed her hand and then left without a word. Macy got up, excited about Rebekah. Not only was she nice, but she was cool too. A successful indie rock band and a tattoo. She was basically the best stepmom ever.

Fake stepmom. Macy rolled her eyes at herself. Now wasn't the time to start thinking about herself as part of this family. It was all a hoax and her goal was still to get back home.

She put on the stiff clothes and grabbed her—Heather's—brush. Her hair felt horrible after not washing it. At least it would be in a bun. She looked around for a mirror, not seeing one. There wasn't even a mirror in the bathroom, which was literally a bath-room. It only had a tub and a small sink.

Did the community think mirrors were evil too?

Macy brushed her hair back as best as she could, sure that it sucked. She could feel lumps on the top of her head. Maybe she would take Rebekah up on her offer to help.

Her stomach jumped around as she thought about starting a new school, even one that was full of kids dressed in white. Maybe that made it worse. Were they going to be nicer or worse than the kids at her real school? Maybe the fact that she was the "daughter" of the future prophet would give her an edge. Maybe she even stood a chance at popularity, whatever that meant in a place like this.

Macy tidied up the room and then went out to the living room, where Rebekah was cooking something on the stove.

"Do you mind if I help you with your hair?" Rebekah asked.

"Please."

Rebekah checked whatever she was cooking and then pulled Macy's bun out. "Where's your brush? Still in your room?" They went back to Macy's room and before long, her hair was done and they were eating breakfast.

Chester spoke excitedly about meeting with Jonah, Abraham, and Isaac that day. Macy couldn't stop thinking about what school would be like, so she could barely pay attention to him. She knew she needed to listen at least a little in case he asked her about it, which he often did, always wanting to make sure she was paying attention to his ramblings. She had learned to listen for key points when he talked without having to actually listen to every word.

"Are you excited about school?" He stared at her.

"I…I guess. I mean, I don't know what to expect."

He looked annoyed.

"I promise to use formal language there. I won't embarrass you."

"That's good to hear."

"You needn't worry too much about it," Rebekah said. "Don't use worldly slang and you should be fine. Everyone has leniency for new members. Also, I've heard your teacher is nice."

Chester and Rebekah exchanged a look.

What did that mean? Macy wasn't going to ask.

"One more thing," Chester said, "remember you don't speak to a male puritan unless spoken to."

Rebekah nodded. "That's one of the most important rules, and also one of the hardest to remember after leaving the world. There are many things that will receive leniency, but that is often not one of them."

"Even kids my own age?"

Chester set his fork down. "Even boys younger than you. Not even a toddler."

Macy's eyes widened, but she kept her thoughts to herself. Guys in the community must have huge heads. Where did they draw the line? Were moms allowed to speak to their sons before spoken to? If not, that was the most ridiculous thing ever.

"Do you understand?"

"Yes." She probably answered too fast, but she didn't want angry Chester to return.

He smiled. "Good. It really shouldn't be that hard. It's just a matter of respect and understanding where you are in the big scheme of things."

Rebekah gave her a reassuring look. "I'll do my best to help you."

Macy looked at her, confused.

"Rebekah is a teacher," Chester said.

"You are?"

"Yes. There are two of us and we sometimes split up the younger kids and the older. If we do that today, I'll be sure to go with your class. My ranking is higher than the other teacher, so it won't be a problem."

"How does the ranking work?"

"You'll learn all about it in school."

Why hadn't she figured that out herself? Had she really expected to study American History and Algebra?

"Are you ready?"

"I just have to go the bathroom—I mean the outhouse."

Chester gave her a serious look. "Hurry. You don't want to make your teacher late, Heather."

Macy got up and went out to the outhouse, hit by the cold. Why didn't they allow coats? There was a thick covering of frost on the ground and she could see her breath. Any sane person would want a thick, warm coat.

When she got back inside, Rebekah was cleaning the last dish. "Are you ready now?"

"I guess."

"You needn't worry. Everyone will like you, Heather."

Macy shrugged.

Rebekah wiped her hands on a towel and then squeezed Macy's shoulders. "You'll do great. No need to be nervous. Let's go."

When they got into the living room, Chester gave Rebekah a big hug and a kiss. Then he turned to Macy. "I wish I could go with you on your first day, Heather, but I need to spend the day with the high prophets. Give me a hug." He opened his arms wide.

Macy walked to him and wrapped her arms around him. He smelled of that awful soap, but then again, she probably did too. He put his arms around her and squeezed tight. "You have a good day, and don't worry. We'll all be back together tonight."

Don't worry? The only part of school she was looking forward to was being away from him.

Finally, he let go and they all went outside and he went the opposite direction as Macy and Rebekah. A lot of people were out, walking around.

"Don't make eye contact with males you don't know. It's considered rude, and if you look at the wrong one, you could end up with a letter on your first day. I'll insist on everyone at school having grace with you, but I have no control over anyone outside of school."

Macy gulped. "What's it like?"

"School, you mean?"

Macy nodded, keeping her eyes low. How was she ever going to remember all of the rules? Just avoid guys altogether?

"It's somewhat like school as you're used to. Desks and books, but instead of learning useless facts which have all been twisted by the world's government, we teach what is actually useful. You'll learn about the community rules, the prophecies, and the professions needed here inside the walls."

At least it was better than being stuck with Chester and his ranting all day. "So, do you celebrate holidays?"

Rebekah shook her head no. "All days are equal. Holidays were dreamed up by the world to meet their evil desires. True happiness comes from appreciating that every day is special. Finding joy in that is something the world will never understand."

"Are there days off? Don't a lot of religions have days to rest?"

"This isn't a religion. It's the truth. Jonah and the other prophets receive messages from up above, teaching us the truisms about this life and the one to come. As for the days off, we do take one day a week to listen to a special message from Jonah and the others, but as you know, we have meetings every evening. We're almost at the school."

Macy looked up, seeing what looked like an old fashioned school house. She held her breath.

School

"**G**OOD MORNING, EVERYONE," Rebekah said, closing the door behind her and Macy.

"Good morning, Teacher," all of the students replied.

Macy looked around, careful not to make eye contact with anyone.

"This is Heather," Rebekah continued. "You remember her from the unveiling ceremony the other night. Many of you know what it's like to be new here, so please be extra helpful. She is not used to our ways yet, although she's been doing very well at home. We are going to start with our copy work this morning, so find the appropriate book of prophecies and begin copying."

Rebekah led Macy to a desk with a cute guy who was busy reading. She told Macy that would be her permanent seat. As Macy sat, Rebekah gathered some books, which were really just stacks of paper held together by string weaved into a binding.

"Start with this one. It's the rules of the community. I'm sure Eve went over the basic ones with you, but to really learn them, you must copy them over and over again."

Macy took the book and ignored the boy next to her. Pretended to ignore him. He was really cute and found herself wanting to stare. He looked to be about her age, and she tried to imagine what he would look like in regular clothes. She couldn't tell which clique he would have been in, but he was adorable with his bright blue eyes and thoughtful expression. And that was saying something since it was hard for anyone to look good in the ugly, white clothes. Maybe that was the point.

"You'll get that copy work done a lot faster if you start," he said.

Macy jumped. She hadn't realized he had been paying any attention to her. "I—uh, yes. You're right." He had spoken to her, so it was okay for her to talk to him, right? But he hadn't given her *permission*. She picked up the large, awkward-shaped pencil sitting in front of her.

"Don't be nervous. It's not so bad here—once you get used to it." He smiled.

Macy could feel her cheeks warm up. "Are you…?"

"From the world? Yes. I've been here a few years, and I have to say that for the most part, the people are a lot nicer. They—uh oh, Teacher is looking our way. Better start writing."

Macy looked up to see Rebekah looking their way. She had a stern look on her face, but she didn't look angry.

Macy looked at the rules and copied them. Most of it she already knew from Eve quizzing her the other day.

After a while, she had to put the pencil down because her hand cramped up. She rubbed it as it protested by hurting even more.

The boy next to her looked up at her, his eyes twinkling. "Used to typing, aren't you?" he whispered.

She nodded.

"It's tough. Don't mention any kind of technology to the adults, but I get it."

"Right. We don't talk about the ways of the world."

He raised his hand.

Rebekah nodded at him.

"Teacher, Heather's hand is cramping. I don't think she's used to so much writing. May I take her outside to walk around and stretch her legs?"

"That's very thoughtful, Luke. Thank you."

"You're welcome, Teacher." He put his pencil down and stood, looking at Macy.

She got up and followed him outside. The sun shone brightly and was warm when she stood directly in it.

"Is it okay with you if we take a walk?" Luke asked.

"As long as it's not against the rules."

Luke laughed, but not in a rude way. "It's fine. We can't be alone in a home, and never near a bedroom, but walking out in plain view is perfectly acceptable."

"Okay."

"Make a fist and then relax your hand. Like this." He held up his hand and showed her, and then looked at her.

Her hand objected, but she made a fist and then let go.

"Good. Keep doing that while we walk around. How do you like the community?"

"Uh, I…well. I haven't really had time to get used to it."

"That's understandable. You were probably in your home all day yesterday for the family honeymoon, right?"

"Pretty much."

"Until you get used to things, you're better off staying quiet and just observing. You seem to be doing that already, so you're already doing well. Before you know it, you'll be used to it here and will have a hard time remembering what it was like before."

She squeezed her hand extra hard, digging her nails into her flesh. "I doubt that." She was going to hold onto every memory of her real family and never let go.

"I sense some animosity. Care to talk about it?"

Macy's heart raced. Did she dare tell him she had been kidnapped? Chester was practically revered by all.

"No pressure," Luke said. "You don't even know me, but if you want to talk with anyone, I'm here and I do know what it's like on the outside. Sure, I don't think about it often anymore, but the memories never leave."

She wanted to tell him, but what if he told Rebekah or Chester? Or someone who would tell them? No. She had to stick to her plan and feel everyone out. She could verbally vomit all over Luke just because he was cute and seemed nice. "Does anyone ever get out of here?"

"Only those who have been set free."

"Set free?" Macy asked, not sure she wanted to know the answer.

"Released from their earthly bodies."

"You mean the only way out of here is to die?"

Luke nodded, giving her an inquisitive look.

"Nobody has ever gotten thrown out?"

"Not that I've ever heard about. Usually, a few punishments is enough to whip anyone into shape."

"Have you ever been punished?"

"That's not usually an appropriate question, but—"

"Sorry."

"You'll find I'm pretty hard to offend. I don't mind answering, but don't go around asking other people. My first month here, I was rude to Jonah. I didn't mean to be, but what's considered rude here is not the same as what we grew up with out there. That night at the community meeting, he brought me up to the front and told everyone what I had said. The entire community called me rude over and over for what felt like hours. Then for the rest of the week, which was only two days, no one was allowed to look at me or talk to me, not even my parents. I had to read the rule books and do a lot of copy work. My hand cramped up really bad, but I wasn't allowed to stop. It took months for my hand to fully recover."

That explained why he was being so kind about her hand cramping. "That's awful."

"It was horrible. But you know what? It taught me what I needed to learn. I haven't gotten into any trouble since then. In the end, it was a blessing."

Macy's eyes widened. She would never let herself get to the point of agreeing that anything like that was good. Treating someone like that was inexcusable. Everyone here may believe the punishments were good things, but she never would. Somehow she would find a way out, but that wouldn't happen if she allowed herself to start thinking like them.

"What do you think of your dad being so close to Jonah? I've never seen Jonah take someone on so soon after their unveiling. No one has ever become a prophet so soon after joining."

"What's so special about that?" she asked.

"Your dad is going to be in the inner circle. No one has been welcomed in the whole time I've been here. It might mean we're moving even closer to entering the Promised Land."

"And that means…?"

"It's our primary goal. The Promised Land is a beautiful, magnificent place where we'll spend the rest of time."

"You really believe that?" Macy asked and then covered her mouth. "Sorry. Don't tell anyone I said that." Images of being shamed and then ignored filled her mind. If she publicly embarrassed Chester, who knew what he would to her? "Please. I didn't mean it."

Luke didn't look bothered. "I didn't believe it for a long time. I understand your hesitation, Heather. I was there. You'll need to get to a place where you believe for yourself."

"Why?"

He stopped and then turned to look at her. "When you're truly a part of the community, you'll receive your true name. You won't be able to enter the Promised Land if you don't have your name."

She stared into Luke's eyes, trying to see if there was a flicker of doubt. She wanted to see it, believing that he was someone she could open up to. If he knew she'd been kidnapped, maybe he could help her escape. If not, she could end up at the wrong end of Chester's fury again.

It was time to play it safe. No one was going anywhere—they were all trapped inside the high, fortressed walls. If she needed to spend weeks feeling people out, she would. She needed to find the right person to open up to. Someone who wouldn't turn her in for claiming that she had been kidnapped by a prophet.

Maybe Luke was that person, but maybe not. She would have to be a hundred percent certain. Chester was sure to have chosen a house with some kind of basement or cellar. He had planned everything out with such precision. There was no way he would leave out a detail like that.

"How does your hand feel?"

"Better."

"We should head back, but first let me see it." Luke took her hand and rubbed it, squeezing hard.

It took all of Macy's self-control not to cry out in pain.

"It's still sore. I'm going to tell Teacher that I think you should rest it for the remainder of the day. Maybe I can take you on field trip. Have you seen the farms yet?"

Macy shook her head.

"Without the farms, we couldn't survive. I can't imagine Teacher disagreeing with a field trip there. What could be more educational than learning about what sustains our way of life?" He turned around and walked toward the school house, still holding onto her hand, rubbing it.

Two men were heading their way, so Macy looked down careful not to even give the impression of making eye contact. She pulled on her hand, sure that the men wouldn't approve of Luke holding it. He wouldn't let go, continuing to squeeze it.

When they crossed paths with the men, Luke stopped, forcing Macy to as well. He gave a slight bow and Macy kept her eyes on the ground, staring at a melting patch of frost.

"What is going on, Luke?"

"Her hand is hurt, so I'm helping. We're heading back to school."

"Carry on." The two men continued walking in the direction they were headed.

Luke tugged on her hand and they followed the path. It was strange that it was okay for him to walk with her, touching her hand. With all the weird, backward rules the community followed, she would have thought that boys and girls would have been expected to walk on different sides of the road, not even allowed to look at each other.

When they got back to the schoolhouse, Luke stopped and rubbed her hand again. "How does that feel?"

"It's still sore."

"Let me rub it a little more." He looked down at her hand and rubbed again. His hand slid and went to her wrist, his fingers resting under her sleeve.

Luke looked into her eyes. He appeared as surprised as she felt. Macy's heart leapt into her throat. Luke's fingers lingered on her wrist, and then he pulled his hand away and cleared his throat.

"We should head back inside." His cheeks were pink.

Macy nodded. What had that been about?

They went inside and Luke told her to go back to the desk while he spoke with the teacher about taking a field trip. Macy rubbed her hand, watching them from the corner of her eyes. She couldn't hear anything they said, but Rebekah kept looking back at her, nodding occasionally.

Macy could feel the stares of other kids, probably because she was the new kid. Or was she the freak again? Not because she was overweight this time, but because her hand hurt and she couldn't keep writing with the pencil. Surely the others like her, the kids who had come from *the world,* would have understood. Who spent hours writing anymore?

Luke sat down and nodded, but didn't say anything.

Rebekah walked to the front of the class and tapped on the chalk board with a ruler. "Excuse me, class. It's almost lunchtime. When we reconvene, some of you are going to take a field trip to a farm. It's been a while since we've had a field trip, and now that we have a new student, the timing is perfect. How many of you, ages twelve and older, are interested?

About half a dozen hands went up.

"Quite a few of you. This is good. We still have some time, so I'm going to take a little walk and let the farmers know to expect you. In the meantime, keep doing your work. I want to see all of your copy work when I return. If you need to, go to the other class and speak with the teacher there."

"Yes, Teacher," said the entire class in unison, minus Macy.

"If the lunch bell rings before I return, you're dismissed to your homes."

Without a word, all the kids went back to their writing, and they didn't slow down when Rebekah left. That would have never happened at her old school. If a teacher ever had to step outside the classroom for even a minute, chaos ensued every time.

Macy made a fist and then extended her fingers. Her hand was still sore, but she decided she better try writing again. She didn't want to get the reputation of being able to get away with things just because she was the teacher's kid—fake kid.

News

THE LIVING ROOM was filled an awkward silence. Chad felt like he should lead the discussion, but he didn't know where to start. Valerie looked to be in a better state of mind than she had the night before.

"Who wants to start?" Chad asked.

Valerie put her face in her hands and then looked up. "I can't deal with this on my own. Times like this, I wish Zoey's dad was around. Maybe if he was, this wouldn't have happened. Honestly, you guys are more family to us than anyone else. I suppose that's why I never thought this would happen. I think of Alex as her brother. She's always been so protective of him, as if he wasn't only Macy's brother, but her own."

Chad looked at Alyssa. "And we should have seen it coming. We grew up best friends and then one day, it became something more. I don't know why we never thought it could happen to Alex."

Alyssa took a step closer to Valerie. "We can all pass the buck, blaming each other or ourselves, but that isn't going fix this. I don't know if anything in our lives can be fixed any more. But what I do know is that nothing needs to be decided now. Let's just be here for our kids—both of them."

Valerie nodded and then turned to Alex. "I'm sorry, Alex. I shouldn't have said those things. I was angry and I'm scared."

He looked down. "I'm sorry too, Ms. Carter. For this whole mess." He looked up and had tears shining in his eyes.

"Oh, Alex." Valerie gave him a hug and then pulled Zoey in. "I hope you guys know I love you, both of you."

"Me too." Alyssa got up and hugged them. "I'm sorry for getting mad, too."

Chad wrapped his arms around all of them. "We'll get through this together."

Valerie nodded. "I'm not okay with this, and I don't agree with keeping the baby, but we can figure that out later. For now we'll just focus on helping you two."

"I couldn't agree more," Alyssa said.

Valerie's phone beeped and she looked at the screen. "I'm glad we were able to have this little talk. I'm sorry to cut it short, but I have to get back to the office."

"I should get back to my blog as well," Chad said. He went to his office and stared at the blank screen. Before Valerie came over, he'd been unable to write anything for his new blog post.

He couldn't write under pressure on a good day, but this was even worse—and not even because of Alex and Zoey's announcement.

The previous afternoon, his boss had brought Chad into his office. Roger hadn't needed to say anything, because Chad knew exactly what was coming from the look on his face. His performance at work had tanked since Macy disappeared.

They had given him a couple weeks off with pay and his coworkers had donated vacation hours so Chad wouldn't have to use his own. But the time since he had returned, he was next to useless and he knew it.

An alert from his computer brought him back to the present. Twelve new friend requests. Why did everyone want to be his friend? Just because his daughter was missing didn't mean he wanted to be friends with everyone who hoped she would return.

He refused to accept the requests, even if it made him look like a jerk. He didn't know any of those people and if they were really interested in Macy, they would just follow his blog. That's where he put everything that he wanted people to know, not on social media. He went to the folder where he kept his copy and paste letters, copied the friend-denial message and pasted it to all twelve of them.

He checked his notifications, got caught up on what everyone was doing—not that he really cared at the moment, but it was a good distraction from what was bothering him. If he couldn't work, then what? His blog made enough to keep Alyssa home, but not him. If he worked at it full time, he would probably be able to pull in enough to keep them both home, but it would take some time.

Chad went back to his blank blog post. What was he supposed to write about? Detective Fleshman had told them not to talk about the phone because they still processing it. What did it matter, though? It had already been all over the news.

What did the phone even mean? They already knew her clothes had been found covered in her blood. Could the phone tell them anything they didn't already know? If they could get some information out of it, they might be able to find out who she had been calling. Maybe they would even find fingerprints. Or would it have been wiped clean?

He wanted answers, but when it came to the police department, it would take longer than he wanted. They simply weren't able to process things any faster than they were.

Chad got up and went to the kitchen for some coffee. Yesterday's still sat in the pot. For a moment he considered warming some up, but ended up rinsing it out and making a fresh batch. Alyssa would probably want some too. He doubted she had gotten any sleep either.

While the pot brewed, he went upstairs to check on her. He found her in the bonus room, asleep on the couch with the news still going. Why did she do that to herself? He found a blanket and covered her up and then turned off the TV. She stirred and then gave him a confused look.

"What's going on?"

"Just turning the news off. Go back to sleep, Lyss."

"Nothing more about the phone?"

He shook his head.

She looked at the time. "You're not going to work?"

"I'm going to work from home today." He had through next week to use that excuse before he told her that he was out of a job.

"Okay." She closed her eyes again.

Chad went to Alex's room. He was sleeping soundly while his alarm beeped next to him.

"Are you going to get up, Alex?"

"Do I have to?" mumbled Alex.

"You've got school and your alarm is blaring."

"Ugh." Alex pulled his pillow from under his head and put it over his face.

Chad pulled the pillow away from him. "Get up. Want me to make you some coffee?"

Alex shot him a dirty look and then turned his alarm off. "Can't I just sleep in? Why do I have to keep going to school?"

"Does repeating the eighth grade sound like fun?"

Alex sat up and grabbed the pillow from Chad. "My sister is missing and I'm going to be a dad at fourteen. Does it matter if I learn about adverbs?"

Chad sat next to Alex. "We have a lot to figure out about the baby. In fact, it's so early in the game that we don't know if it will last. Do you know how many pregnancies end in miscarriage early on?"

"You're a jerk."

"I'll ignore that. I'm being realistic. Your mom practically lived in fear until she hit a certain point. And even if Zoey does end up having it, wouldn't you two give it up for adoption? Give the baby the best chance possible. There are lots of nice couples who can't have kids, Alex."

"That doesn't change anything. I'll still be a dad. The baby will still be mine even if someone else raises him."

Chad took a deep breath. "All I'm trying to say is that skipping school isn't going to help you. Getting an education is the best thing you can—"

"No, it's not. That's the lies your generation was told. Look at all the people out there with college debt flipping burgers. My generation doesn't want that. *I* don't want that."

"You're not going into debt in middle school. Where did you hear that, anyway?"

Alex rolled his eyes. "I don't want to have this conversation. Look, I'll go to school so you'll get off my back. Deal?"

"I'm not trying to irritate you. But it's important that you go to school."

"There's such a thing as summer school. Who better to do that than me? No one has a better excuse for missing school."

"You really want to spend your summer in school?"

"Forget it!" Alex got up and grabbed some clothes before storming out of his room.

Chad looked around the empty room and picked some of the mess off the floor, putting things on the chair for Alex to organize later. When he got into the hall, he could hear the shower.

Why was it so hard to get along with Alex these days? Chad thought things would improve after their talk the night they found out about the pregnancy, but it looked like it would take more than that.

Alex and Chad had gotten along so well when Alex was younger. In fact, Alex wouldn't leave him alone for a minute, always wanting his attention. It had been annoying at the time, but looking back, his heart ached. Was it possible to get close again? Or was all lost for the teen years?

The landline rang. Chad sighed. The only people that called that number anymore were solicitors and his in-laws. He went down to the kitchen and checked the caller ID. The police department?

"Hello?"

"Chad, this is Detective Fleshman again."

He hated that they talked with him so much they used his first name. "What is it? Why are you calling this line?"

"We called both of your cell numbers, but neither one was answered."

Chad felt his pocket, but it was empty. "What is it, Detective?"

"We need you and Alyssa to come down to the station."

"Again? I thought everything was squared away with the phone."

"This isn't about the cell phone. There's a possible new clue and we want to talk with you before the news gets a hold of this." The detective's voice was solemn.

Chad leaned against the nearest wall. "What do you mean?"

"Just get down here as soon as possible. The shift change is coming up and I want my team to tell you two."

"I'll wake Alyssa."

"Thank you, Chad."

He hung up and stared at the coffee. Why did the detective sound so serious? He took a deep breath. He needed to calm down before he talked to Alyssa, or he would freak her out. He poured some coffee and drank it black.

Maybe they just needed them go downtown for something routine.

He could convince Alyssa of that, but he knew better.

Chad heard footsteps. Alex appeared and glared at him.

"Want me to make you some breakfast?" Chad asked.

"You're a jerk."

"Still?"

"Why'd you go through my stuff?" Alex's eyebrows came together.

"Go through...? I didn't go through anything. I cleared a path to the door."

Alex folded his arms. "Leave me alone." He turned around and ran out the front door.

Chad walked to where he could see outside, and watched Alex walk to the bus stop where a group of kids were already waiting. At least Alex would be at school while he and Alyssa were at the station. He drank the rest of his coffee and headed back to the bonus room. She was still sleeping on the couch. He hated to wake her, but what choice did he have?

Crushed

ALYSSA AND CHAD sat holding hands in the police station waiting room.

"What's taking them so long?" Alyssa asked. She pushed the heel of her boot against the leg of her chair trying to squash the horrible thoughts forcing their way into her mind.

Chad squeezed her hand. "This might be good news."

Had he lost his mind? She gave him a look that told him how she felt.

"Think about it. When they found Macy's clothes they rushed us in, remember? If they're making us wait, it can't be that urgent. It could be good news."

What was wrong with him? Was he just talking to hear himself speak? She gave him an annoyed look.

"Well, so far they haven't found anything indicating that she's come to any harm."

"Yeah, but you know what they say about the first twenty-four hours," Alyssa said.

"I can think of several famous kidnapping cases where kids were found alive months and even years later."

"So you think she was kidnapped now? You don't think she just ran away?"

Chad gave her an exasperated look. "I was just giving you a worst case scenario that turned out well."

"This really isn't the time for worst case statistics. I know which ones you're referring to and they were forced to live as young wives for sick, old men. I can't let myself think about that happening to Macy."

"That didn't happen each time. I'm just—"

"Mr. and Mrs. Mercer."

Officer Reynolds stood by the front desk. He gave them a weak smile and tipped his cap. "We're ready for you two."

Even though Alyssa was still irritated with Chad, she held his hand as they followed Reynolds to a back room. Detective Fleshman and Officer Anderson came into the room as Chad and Alyssa were getting seated.

Chad looked at them. "What's going on? Is it the phone?"

Fleshman shook his head. "We don't know what to make of that, but that's now why we asked you to come down here."

Chad's face clouded over. "Why are we here then?"

Alyssa noticed that the three policemen's faces were solemn. "Is something wrong?"

Anderson nodded and then sat down next to Alyssa. "We needed to see you right away because it's going to be everywhere soon."

"What?" Alyssa demanded. "What is it?"

Looking back and forth at them, Anderson cleared his throat. "A body has been found."

Alyssa gasped. Tears filled her eyes and spilled out. She shook. He had to be lying or wrong, or both.

Reynolds knelt next to her. "No one knows if it's her. The body—we can't identify the face."

Chad stood up, letting go of Alyssa's hand. "What does *that* mean?" He was practically shouting.

Fleshman walked in front of him and spoke in a soothing tone. "The body was found in Clearview. We haven't seen it, but it's coming directly here to rule out it being Macy. Our team will check it against dental records and we'll move on from there."

"But what does that *mean*?" Chad repeated.

Alyssa felt cold, and she couldn't stop shaking. "Wh…when will we know?"

"That's our top priority, but at the same time, we're going to quadruple-check every step of the process. Another thing: just because the body can't be identified by the face that doesn't mean that we can't use other markers. Does she have any identifying marks that would help? Birth marks? Tattoos or piercings?"

Unable to deal with the thought of Macy's *body*, Alyssa put her face into her hands, sobbing. Someone put a hand on her shoulder and she was vaguely aware of Chad speaking.

They had to be wrong—they just had to be. It couldn't be Macy. No. She was safe somewhere, even though they didn't know where.

The air felt like it was crushing Alyssa from all sides. She struggled to breathe. What if it *was* Macy? Was that why they had found next to no clues up until now? She gulped for air, still shaking.

Something touched her back. It was probably Chad's hand, but instead of being a comfort, it felt like he was pushing her further into the suffocating nothingness around her.

Alyssa jumped up, looking around the room. She couldn't focus on anything, barely even aware that she was at the police station. Oxygen was lacking, and she felt light-headed.

The others surrounded her. They appeared to be talking, but she couldn't hear anything over the sounds of her fear. She threw her hands out in front of her.

Was someone screaming?

It was her.

Tears ran down her face, pouring like never before. They ran down her neck, drenching her shirt's collar. Chad's arms wrapped around her, and she fought him.

Alyssa may have still been screaming, but she couldn't tell. She had to get out of there and find Macy. Why hadn't they looked harder?

She wouldn't be able to go on if Macy was…she couldn't even think the word.

Officer Reynolds was inches from her. His mouth was moving, but she still couldn't hear anything. They were wrong—whatever body they found, it wasn't her child. It belonged to someone else.

Her stomach and chest felt like they were going to simultaneously explode and implode. She gave into the weakness overtaking her, and she went limp in Chad's arms.

She was vaguely aware of him readjusting himself, trying to keep hold of her. Soft, rich oxygen filled her lungs and the sounds of talking around her filled her ears. Chad held her tightly, running his hands over her hair.

The sounds of speaking slowly formed into words she could comprehend. Alyssa couldn't make enough sense of them to understand what they were saying.

She continued to suck in the air around her, filling her lungs, and starting to feel more normal. She still wasn't getting enough air.

Random thoughts ran through her mind. Everything from memories of Macy as a toddler to her last status update, saying that she'd run away. Images from news broadcasts, pondering every possibility—many of them had given her plenty of nightmares.

Someone said her name. Alyssa looked up, unsure of who was speaking to her. The room had stopped spinning and the sounds around her were natural. She still couldn't process what anyone was saying. Facts and images from Macy's disappearance ran through her mind, taking up most of her awareness.

Her mind felt like a computer, trying to make sense of what she knew. She was trying to find any clue that could prove her daughter was alive and well, even if they couldn't get to her.

Alyssa looked up, finally able to find her voice. "Wait. Our dentist's office burned down. It was on the news."

Fleshman raised an eyebrow, stepping closer. "That was your dentist?"

"I'll look into it," Anderson said. "I'll see if they stored their files online. You never know around here."

"You mean we might never know if it's Macy?" Chad asked, sounding agitated.

"There are other ways. DNA testing would be possible. But we always go for the simplest solution. Usually facial recognition is where we start, but since we can't do that…."

Alyssa put her hands back over her face, tuning them out. Was it possible the girl found in Clearview was Macy? That was pretty far away and she couldn't imagine her daughter going there—there was nothing there. Unless that was where the boy was from, if he even existed.

She heard something about Alex and looked up again. "What about Alex?"

Reynolds looked at her. "We can pick him up from school for you if you'd like."

"Why?"

"So you can tell him before he hears it from school. All the kids have the Internet on their phones. All it takes is one kid hearing the news and it'll spread to everyone."

"No." Alyssa stood. "He doesn't need to be picked up by the police. As much as we appreciate everything you've done, he doesn't need it. Kids are cruel. They'll jump to the worst conclusion and run with it. He's been through enough. We'll get him."

"Are you okay to drive?" Anderson asked. "You just found out startling news."

"I have to be there for Alex. We can't let him hear about this at school, by some little jerk who just wants to see him react." Alyssa stood tall, trying to prove that she was able to get her son from school.

Chad took her hand in his, still holding her close. "She's right. We'd better call Valerie too, so she can decide whether or not to pick up Zoey."

Still shaking, Alyssa squirmed out of Chad's hold and took out her cell phone. She tried to dial Valerie's number, but wasn't able to keep her finger steady.

Detective Fleshman gave her a concerned look. "If you can't even make a call, I don't want to send you anywhere in a car."

"I'll do it." Chad snatched the phone out of Alyssa's hands. He swiped around the screen. "Valerie? This is Chad." He explained the situation to her and then handed it back to Alyssa when he was done. "See? We're fine to pick up the kids. I'm fine to drive."

"How soon until the news finds out?" asked Alyssa.

Reynolds gave her an apologetic look. "Not long. They're vultures."

In the car, Alyssa asked if they were picking up Zoey too. "In there, you said we were picking up the kids."

He turned right. "Yeah. Valerie can't get away from work, so she said she would call the school and give permission for us to get her."

"I'm surprised she trusts us."

Chad put his hand on her knee. "You know she didn't mean the things she said the other day. We were all freaked out, and especially after everything we've gone through lately with Macy."

Alyssa's eyes filled with tears again. "And now this. Do you think it's her?"

"Honestly, I think it's a long shot. Clearview? Do you know how many kids go missing every day? A lot."

"But if she was taken against her will, she could have gone anywhere. By now she could be on the other side of the world." Alyssa's voice wavered so much she couldn't continue.

"That's just it. She could be anywhere—why Clearview?"

"Do they know what happened to the girl? I was too upset to listen to everything they said."

"Not until they do the autopsy. Some jogger found her." He pulled into the school and parked in the lot that adjoined the high school and middle school. "Do you want me to get both of them? Or should we split up?"

"I'll get Alex. I need to see my baby. I need to know at least one of my children is safe and sound."

"All right. I'll get Zoey." He gave her a kiss. "Don't worry. That body isn't Macy. She's safe—I can feel it. We'll get her back, alive and well."

Alyssa gave him a doubtful look. He didn't know any more than anyone else. She pulled down the sun visor to check the mirror. She hadn't put on any makeup so there was nothing smeared across her face from crying. Her hair was messed up, so she attempted to fix it before getting out of the car.

As she walked to the middle school campus, she went over what to say to Alex. He would know something was wrong since he was being picked up so early. He was probably only in his first or second class of the day.

How would they ever tell their son the news about the body? He was as upset as she was about Macy just being gone. She knew how he was feeling without him saying a word. It had been that way since he was a baby.

For some reason, Macy had always been harder to read. If Alex had been the one planning to run away, she would have figured it out. Why had it always been so difficult with Macy? It wasn't like they had a bad relationship, but it didn't come as naturally as with Alex.

Why hadn't she tried harder? If she would have put out more effort to figure Macy out, even though it was challenging at times, would Macy have disappeared? Could she have done something to prevent all of this heartache?

When she got to the office, the secretary told her that Alex was already on his way.

"Why? Is he okay?"

She nodded. "The detective called and said that you would be on your way. You know, my heart aches for everything you guys are going through. Our family prays for you guys every night. I don't know how you guys do it."

Tears stung at Alyssa's eyes. "Me neither."

Lunch

A BELL SOUNDED from somewhere outside. It reminded Macy of a church bell tower. The sounds of pencils being set on desks surrounded her, followed by the scuffle of chairs pushed under desks. A light murmur of conversation filled the room, surprising her. It was the first time she had heard most of them speak.

She put her pencil down and got up. She followed the kids outside and looked around for Rebekah. Where was she? Was she supposed to come back? Macy wasn't sure she remembered how to get back to their house. They had taken several turns and everything looked the same to her.

"Are you all right?" asked Luke. "You look lost."

"I don't see Re—Teacher. I thought she would walk home with me."

"You don't remember the way back?"

Macy shook her head.

"Do you want me to wait with you or show you the way?"

"You know where I live?"

"When you live within the confines of a fence, you learn where everything is. I could take you to any house or place of business."

"Do you think she's coming back here or going straight home after speaking with the farmers?"

"She didn't say."

Macy knew that. That's why she asked him. She bit back an irritated comment. If she made the wrong choice, she could piss off Chester and find herself locked up somewhere. "Do you think I should wait for her?"

"I'd hate for you to miss lunch. Why don't I take you to your house? We know she'll go there to eat if she comes back here to find it empty."

"Okay."

"How does your hand feel? I saw you were writing again."

"It's pretty sore, but I'll live."

Luke made friendly conversation as they walked along the streets. A lot of people walked around.

"Does everyone stop what they're doing to have lunch?" Macy asked.

"Yes. Everything stops while people eat and do light household chores. Some even take naps or relax. It depends on the family. We take a couple hours to rest in the middle of the day. It helps everyone to be more productive in the afternoon. Here's your street."

Macy looked around. "How can you tell the difference between the houses?"

He laughed. "Yours has that little patch of flowers by the porch. See?"

She squinted, looking at each of the porches until she found a small patch of flowers. "I see it."

"Have a nice lunch. I'd better hurry home. My mother will wonder where I've gone."

"Thanks for everything."

Luke smiled. "No problem, Heather. See you in a couple hours." He walked off with a little wave.

Macy went to the house with flowers, nervous that it was the wrong one. What if there was more than one house with purple flowers near the porch? When she opened the door, she recognized everything inside.

She heard some noise coming from the kitchen.

"Rebekah, is that you?" called Chester.

"It's Heather."

Chester came out of the kitchen, looking confused. "Where's your mom?"

"She had to do an, uh, errand for school."

His eyebrows furrowed. "So you had to walk home yourself?"

"No. Another student came with me."

"That wasn't very considerate of her. It's your first day and you don't know your way around here. She should have—"

"She was looking into something for me. My hand—"

"Don't interrupt, Heather." Chester's lips curved downward. "I'll need to talk with her. This is unacceptable."

Macy's heart sank. "She didn't do anything wrong. She was trying to help me."

"There's no reason for you to protect her. She's an adult, and she should have been watching out for you."

"But she was. She—"

"Stop. Not another word. Get lunch ready." He walked past her and opened the wood stove, poking at the embers.

"She was talking with—"

"I said not another word. Or did you not hear me?" He turned around, giving her a scary look.

Macy turned around and went into the kitchen, her heart pounding. She should have waited for Rebekah at the school. Why hadn't she thought it through? She should have known that Chester would get angry over not coming home with Rebekah.

He wouldn't turn his anger on Rebekah, would he? She was his new wife of only a couple days. Surely, he wouldn't. Except that she couldn't trust him in the slightest. Tears filled her eyes. Rebekah had been nothing but nice to Macy, and now Macy felt like she had betrayed Rebekah. She was so sweet. There was no way she would see his rage coming.

Macy pulled leftovers out of the icebox, almost without thinking. She had to find a way to protect Rebekah. It was all Macy's fault that Chester was angry. She should have just waited at school. It was so obvious now; why hadn't it been earlier?

She pulled out a pot and poured the contents into it. Then she wiped her eyes, removing the tears. When Chester saw weakness, he took advantage of it. She had to show him that she wasn't upset.

He turned around when she approached. His eyebrows came together. "I would have chosen the food from two nights ago so it won't go bad as fast, but I suppose this will do since it's already out." He stared into her eyes for a moment before snatching the pot from her. "I didn't hear the water run. I suppose you didn't wash your hands first, did you?"

Heart pounding in her ears, she shook her head.

"Figures." He slammed the pot onto the top of the wood stove. "Germs! They still exist out here. People still get sick from stupidity like that. Yes, everyone is a lot healthier here, but it's not because bacteria ceases to exist. You have to wash your hands when you prepare food. Always!"

Macy stepped back. "I forgot. I'll go wash them now."

"What's the point?"

She stared at him, knowing that whatever she said would be wrong.

"Just go to your room and wait for your mom to return."

"I have to go to the bathroom."

"I don't care. Just wash your hands after that. Do I need to spell everything out for you? Do I need to do your thinking for you?"

Macy shook her head.

"I should hope not. There are basic things in life that I shouldn't have to worry about. Things you should just do because they're common sense. If I have to think for you I will, but I have more important things to do."

A lump formed in her throat. She nodded, afraid that if she anything she would burst into tears.

"Just go!"

She ran out of the room, through the kitchen, and to the outhouse. The tears finally spilled out when she got outside. By the time she sat down, she was sobbing. She hadn't meant to upset him. If she would have known he would react like that, she would have just waited for Rebekah to return. Why was she so stupid?

Macy thought she heard the front door of the house. Or was it the door from another house? The wood walls of the outhouse were so thin, she could hear everything outside. That made her self-conscious, knowing people could probably hear her when she was in there.

When she got in the house, Chester was standing in front of the wood stove, his arms crossed. He didn't look her way, much to her relief. She also didn't see Rebekah. Was that good or bad? Surely that wouldn't have been enough time for him to hurt her.

She closed the door behind her as quiet as possible and then washed her hands in the ice-cold water in the sink. She wasn't going to go near him to warm it on the stove.

Just as she was walking through the living room, the front door opened. Was there any way for Macy to warn Rebekah about Chester's mood?

Rebekah smiled, looking back and forth between the two of them. Obviously, she wasn't yet aware of the tension filling the room. Rebekah held up a small box. "I brought fresh berries."

"Where were you?" Chester demanded.

She looked startled at his tone, but didn't react. "I needed to speak with the farmers because our class is taking a field trip this afternoon. It will help Heather to get acquainted with how the community is run. Farmer Daniel let me pick a box berries for us. Wasn't that nice?"

Chester knocked the box from her hands. It hit the wall and blueberries rolled in all directions.

Rebekah looked shocked. "What—?"

"Why didn't you walk back with Heather?"

She stood back, not stepping on any berries. "When I returned to the school, everyone was already gone. The other teacher told me that Luke had walked her home."

"A *boy* walked her home?" Chester stepped closer to Rebekah.

"It was perfectly appropriate. The streets are always full at the lunch bell."

"Heather is never to be alone with a boy, do you understand? Ever."

She nodded. "I do now."

"Good. Now pick up those berries and wash them off. Lunch is almost ready."

Macy went over to the berries and scooped up a handful.

Chester glared at her. "I told your mom to pick those up. You go to your room."

"I just want to help."

"If *I* wanted you to help, I would have told you. I did no such thing. To your room."

Macy gave Rebekah an apologetic look and then went to her room. She was shaking as she closed the door. Why had she let her guard down? Why had she been dumb enough to think his good mood would last? His anger had probably been simmering underneath, just waiting for the opportunity—any excuse—to be released.

She heard him chewing out Rebekah. He wasn't yelling, but his voice was raised and he was being just as mean to her as he had been to Macy many times.

Pacing the room, she wiped tears from her face. Macy threw herself on the bed, crying into the pillow. Now Rebekah would probably hate her. Then her only friend would be Luke, if Chester didn't forbid Macy from ever speaking to him again.

Her door opened and Chester came in. "Lunch is ready. Get up and eat with us. If you haven't washed your hands yet, be sure to. Nobody needs to get sick and die because of you."

Macy sat up, using the bed covering to wipe her face. It was probably red and puffy, but she couldn't do anything about that. She wasn't about to splash ice-cold water on her face.

She took a deep breath and went to the kitchen, preparing herself for whatever might be in store. When she got there, both Rebekah and Chester were already eating, facing their plates.

She would have felt a lot better if Rebekah would have looked at her, but she didn't. Not that Macy could blame her. She had pretty much betrayed her.

Waiting

ZOEY CLUNG TO Alex's hand in the backseat. She knew by the look on his face that he was as worried as she was. Their parents had been so insistent that they get back to school, and now they were pulling them out before lunch? That didn't make any sense...unless something was wrong. Really wrong. And judging by Alyssa's red, puffy eyes, something was.

Neither Chad nor Alyssa said anything. It was obvious that they were waiting to tell them the news until they got home. The silence felt like a heavy weight. Zoey was sure that if she said anything, something would break. Probably Alyssa.

The only thing that made any sense was that there was bad news about Macy. That made Zoey sick to her stomach.

She squeezed Alex's hand. Her protective nature wanted to wrap her arms around him and tell him that everything would be all right. But would it?

A lump formed in her throat. Surely Chad and Alyssa wouldn't be driving them home so calmly if Macy was dead. They'd be freaking out. Whatever the news was, it wasn't that.

Zoey leaned her head against Alex's shoulder. He was shaking. She tried to scoot closer to him, but couldn't because of the seat belt.

Her head hurt horribly, and she wanted a cigarette. No, she needed one. That would fix her headache and calm her down. But she couldn't have one, even though she knew the withdrawals would get worse. She couldn't give the kid that kind of a start in life. If that was the only thing she could give him or her, that would be it.

They pulled into the Mercer's driveway. Zoey took her belt off and wrapped her arms around Alex, squeezing him tight. "Everything's going to be okay."

"Have you seen my mom? This can only mean one thing." Tears shone in his eyes.

"It can mean lots of things, Alex. More clothes found, maybe."

He shook his head.

"Come on, you two." The solemn tone of Chad's voice sent chills down Zoey's back.

She grabbed her bag and pulled Alex out of the car. Zoey noticed a police cruiser pulling in across the street. Had they followed them? Or were they just arriving to watch the house? It couldn't be a coincidence that they arrived at the same time.

Zoey's heart dropped. Maybe Chad and Alyssa did have the news that she and Alex were dreading.

Her stomach twisted in tight knots as she walked to the house. Zoey expected Macy to open the door, and she wanted to punch herself. She knew better than to expect to Macy.

The sinking feeling in her gut told her she was about to find out if she would she ever see her best friend again.

When they got inside, Alex threw his bag on the floor and glared at his parents. "What's going on? You brought us—"

"Let's sit." Chad walked to the living room.

Alex looked like he was going to have a nervous breakdown, so Zoey put her arm around him and helped him onto the couch. Alyssa sat at Alex's feet and put her hands on his knees. She wouldn't look either of them in the eyes.

Chad pulled another chair up, sitting about a foot in front of Zoey. He took a deep breath. "It's important we tell you two what's going on before you hear it anywhere else."

Zoey's heart picked up speed, almost feeling as though it had jumped into her throat.

"There's no reason to believe this has anything to do with Macy, but we have to prepare ourselves for gossip." He explained about body that had been found, again reminding them that there was no proof that it was Macy.

As Zoey tried to process what Chad was saying, she looked over at

Alex. Large tears fell into his lap and his lips wavered. She held him closer, leaning her head against his. He was shaking even worse now.

Alyssa rested her forehead on his knees. She was crying too.

Chad was saying something about dental records, but Zoey couldn't focus. The lump in her throat was twice the size it had been, but the tears wouldn't come. She wanted to cry along with her boyfriend and her best friend's mom, but she couldn't.

She buried her face into Alex's side, not wanting anyone to see that she wasn't crying. It wasn't that she didn't care—she did, more than anything. In fact, she couldn't stop blaming herself. Why hadn't she gone with Macy to meet Jared? She could've left them alone after meeting and threatening him to be nice, but she hadn't been there for her best friend.

All she'd been able to think about at the time was that she couldn't go on a double date because she was in love with Alex. She had been afraid of Macy kicking her out of her life.

Zoey was a coward. *That* was why Macy was gone.

She shook, angry with herself and finally tears came. Someone put an arm around her. Zoey looked over to see Chad with his arms around both her and Alyssa. They were all in a huddle, sobbing together.

The house phone rang a few times and eventually Chad went to get it.

"It's not her, right?" Zoey asked, wiping her eyes. "The body, I mean." She knew she had makeup smeared all over her face because it got all over her hands. She looked at Alex's shirt and saw it smeared on there too.

"Let's hope not." Alyssa wiped at her eyes.

Alex sniffled. "When will we know?"

"I don't know, baby. They said something about checking dental records, but our dentist's office burned down. If she's...she's...." Alyssa's eyes shone with tears and she put her head back down, shaking.

Zoey and Alex shared a look of helplessness. What could they possibly say? It was obvious that Alex wanted to comfort his mom, but he couldn't even help himself, much less her.

"What would she be doing all the way in Clearview?" Zoey asked. "Think about it. She wouldn't go there. There's not even decent shopping." She had hoped the last comment would at least get someone to crack a smile, but it hadn't worked.

Alyssa looked up. "We can only hope."

Alex wiped his eyes. "But they have enough to think it might be her, right? Why else would they have told you?"

"They wanted us to hear it from them first and not the news. In fact, we probably want to avoid watching the news altogether." Alyssa sighed.

Chad came back and sat next to Alyssa.

"Who was that?" asked Alyssa.

He shook his head. "It's already hit the national news. Everyone wants to hear from us."

Alyssa's eyes filled with tears again. "Why do they need to? Can't they just leave us alone for once?"

Chad kissed the top of her head. "And that's why Anderson said he would give our statement as our family's representative."

She let out a sigh of relief.

"I told Anderson to direct people to my blog if they have any questions. Of course that means I'm going to have to write up something about this 'latest development' as they're calling it." He frowned.

"You shouldn't have to deal with that, Chad. They should just leave us alone—completely."

He looked away. "I do need the added traffic. I have to get more income from the blog now."

Alyssa gave him a confused look. "Are you not telling me something?"

Chad grimaced, looking directly at her. "I haven't been able to do my work at the levels of quality it needs to be...."

"What are you saying?"

"I'm being let go."

Alyssa's mouth dropped open. "When were you going to tell me?"

"There's been so much going on—more pressing matters."

She put her face into her hands. "What are we going to do? Are we going to lose the house?" She looked, staring at him. "We can't lose this house. This is the last place we saw Macy. This is where her stuff is—her room! Exactly how she left it." More tears spilled onto her cheeks. "I won't lose this house. Ever."

He put his hand on her arm, but she pushed it away.

"Listen to me, Lyss. They're giving me a generous severance package. I have time to work on the blog. Maybe we'll have to give up cable and movie streaming for a while, but we'll make it work." He paused. "We aren't going to lose the house."

Alyssa narrowed her eyes, but looked like she wanted to believe him.

"I promise," he said.

Alex sat up, causing Zoey to readjust herself. "Dad, I have an idea. What if I write an open letter to Macy? If you post it on your blog, do you think people would read it? Would it help with your click-throughs or whatever?"

Chad looked thoughtful. "That's a great idea, Alex. Not just for my stats, but just for you to write it."

Zoey cleared her throat. "I can write one too."

"That would be perfect, Zoey. Thank you. Not only would the world love to hear from you two, but like I said, I think it would be good for you guys. Maybe we could all do that. What do you think, Lyss?"

Her lips shook. "I don't know if I can."

"You don't?"

She shook her head. "I can't say goodbye. I won't."

"Mom," Alex said. "It's not that. I'm going to write mine hoping that Macy finds it and reads it. Maybe she'll decide to come back."

"Me too." Zoey nodded. "Macy would want to hear from you too. Maybe I can get some of her other friends to write letters too. Think of how she would feel if she was out there and read those? It could be a 'begging Macy to come back' campaign. We can let her know that no matter what the news says, we haven't stopped believing."

Alyssa nodded, taking a deep breath. "When you put it that way, how could I not?"

Locked

MACY HEARD SOMETHING shoved against the bedroom door. Chester was locking her in there for the rest of the day. Rebekah had been ordered to return to school not speaking about Macy's whereabouts. Chester didn't want anyone to have the impression that he couldn't control his family. Not when he was working so closely with Jonah and the other prophets.

Macy looked at the window, already knowing that it was nailed shut.

"Don't make a sound while I'm away. Do you hear me?" Chester called.

"Yes."

"Good. I'll be back when I get back. If your mom gets here before me, you're not to leave the room. Even if she opens the door. Am I understood?"

"Yes." Macy sat on her bed, listening to the sounds of his footsteps. First, he went up and down the hall and then he went into the living room. She heard the squeak of the fire stove door opening followed by a sizzling sound. Had he put the fire out with water? The house would freeze without that.

Of course he wouldn't want her comfortable while being punished. In fact, she was surprised that she was allowed in her room. He probably had something else in mind for when she really acted up.

This was just a warning.

Finally, she heard the front door close. She peeked through the curtain and watched as he walked away. It looked like he was talking to himself. Big surprise. He loved the sound of his own voice.

Even though she was locked in the room, it was a relief to be away from him. She actually would have preferred to go to the school with Rebekah. It had been so nice to talk with Luke, although it didn't look like that was going to happen again. After Chester's tantrum, Rebekah would be sure to keep Macy away from all boys.

Maybe Macy could find a way to speak with him when Rebekah wasn't looking. Surely there would have to be times that could happen. They shared a desk; they would have to speak sometimes.

It seemed like Luke had wanted to say more to her, and Macy intended to find out what. Would he be willing to find a way out of the community? It couldn't be sealed perfectly tight. If people could escape Alcatraz, then it had to be possible to get out of this place.

Or was she dreaming too big? Was she making too much out of her interaction with Luke? She sat on the bed, going over every detail of their interaction.

Even if she wasn't able to talk with Luke again, Chester couldn't stop her from making friends with the girls, could he?

The worst part was that she didn't know what would set him off. Even Rebekah, who was obviously a dedicated member of the community, hadn't expected him to be angry about Macy talking with a boy. If she knew the rules and he still caught her off guard, what would throw him into his next rage?

Macy would have to be extremely careful. Sometimes he blew up over such insignificant things that the only explanation was he wanted to explode, and took any excuse he could find.

That was it.

Maybe he wasn't mad about Luke at all. What if he'd had a frustrating morning with Jonah and the other prophets? If any of them had said or done anything to embarrass him, it would've been enough to send him into a fit. But being that he wanted to impress them, he wouldn't have taken it out on them.

He would have waited until he got home, looking for the first halfway reasonable excuse.

That would explain him blowing up about Luke.

Macy got up and walked around the room. How long was Chester going to leave her in there? Until dinner? Until the nightly meeting? He wouldn't leave her locked up through that. *Everyone* was expected to be at the meeting. Except maybe those who were being shamed. Macy wasn't sure about that.

Chester had sounded bent on keeping the "indiscretion" a secret, so maybe he was worried about what everyone thought of him that he would actually protect Macy from a shaming.

Something could be heard outside. It sounded like it was in their yard. Macy moved aside the curtain and saw someone walking toward their house. She narrowed her eyes, focusing. It was hard to tell with everyone wearing white. It was a woman, Macy could tell because of the bun.

Whoever it was walked right through the front door. Why not? There was no lock.

Did the lady even know that Macy was there? Or was she coming just to see her? Footsteps sounded like they were headed her way. Macy's heart raced. She backed away from the door, pushing herself against the dresser. Her breath caught as she heard something scrape against the hall.

Whoever it was, she was moving whatever Chester had pushed against her door. Macy looked around for something to grab if she needed to fight. She saw some scissors and took them, holding them behind her back.

The doorknob turned and Macy looked for a place to hide. There was no wasted space in the room giving her any place to slide under or behind. Her pulse beat in her ears, drowning out the sound of the door opening.

She shook as the door opened. It took her a moment to register that Eve stood in the doorway.

"What...what are you doing here?" Macy asked, nearly out of breath.

Eve smiled. "Good afternoon, Heather. I thought you could use some company."

Macy squeezed the scissors. "How did you know I was in here?"

"Your dad mentioned that you could use some guidance."

"He did?"

She smiled, not coming any closer. "He did. I'm sorry you had a rough morning. Can I see your hand?"

Her hand? Right, her sore hand. "Sure." Macy set the scissors down as quietly as possible, and walked toward Eve holding out her right hand.

Eve took her hand and looked it over. "It does look a bit swollen. I don't think it requires staying home from school, although it is your dad's call as head of the household." She stared into Macy's eyes.

Macy didn't say anything, but she held Eve's gaze, not wanting to appear guilty. She hadn't done anything wrong.

"I want to show you something. Is that all right with you?"

Macy's heart sank. Was this going to be worse than being locked up?

"You're not in trouble, dear Heather. It's going to help you find understanding."

That didn't help her to feel any better. But what other option did she have? She nodded.

"Good. Do you need to use the toilet before we leave? I don't imagine that you were able to use it before I got here."

"Yes."

"I'll wait for you in the living room." Eve turned and left the room.

Letting out a silent sigh of relief, Macy followed her, but then went through the kitchen when Eve went into the main room and stood in front of the wood stove, holding her hands in front of it. *Good luck warming up*, Macy thought.

When she got outside, Macy noticed that the temperature had dropped since she had been out last. She hurried into the outhouse, which wasn't much warmer, and went back inside. She was sure to wash her hands in the sink, aware of their obsession with cleanliness.

Eve smiled at her again when she came into the living room. "Are you ready?"

Macy paused, wishing she had a coat to take with her. Why did they insist on walking around in the cold winter without them? Didn't people get sick or worse, die? There was a reason that people wore coats, and it wasn't fashion. Not in the snow.

"Come on."

Macy hurried and went outside with Eve, shivering as soon as the frosty air hit her skin. She struggled to keep up with Eve who was walking fast—because of the cold? Or was it because she thought she was important, being married to the head prophet?

They went down several streets before they stopped in front of an odd-shaped building. It was almost round. Macy followed Eve around to the other side to a door.

Eve opened the door, but didn't go in. Macy gave her a questioning look.

"You need to go in on your own."

"Why?"

"Going in there, you'll find what you're looking for. If you're blessed, you'll see a vision into your future. Not everyone does their first time, but being Chester's daughter, I wouldn't be surprised in the least if you did. Go on."

Macy looked back and forth between Eve and the doorway. She couldn't see anything inside.

"Hurry, before it gets dark. And take this." Eve pulled out a candle, lighting it without even putting the candle down. She handed it to Macy.

Macy's throat felt dry as she took the candle.

"I'll be waiting out here for you. Take as long as you need."

Macy took a deep breath and walked toward the door, her pulse quickening.

When she entered the building, she gasped in horror.

Visions

MACY STARED AT the room, afraid to go inside. She held her breath and shook, this time it wasn't due to the chilly air.

Eve pushed her forward and then closed the door behind her.

The room was mostly dark, but the candle lit it better than she had expected because every inch of the walls and ceiling were covered in thousands of mirrors. She looked around, seeing herself and the candle flame everywhere she looked. The mirrors were of every size imaginable, each one reflecting off each other.

She didn't just see one image of her, she saw many. Why had Eve brought her there? Was this some kind of torture? The candle and her white garb made the room even creepier. It reminded her of a scary movie—which was probably where Jonah had gotten the idea for this place.

Had Eve been serious when she said that Macy might have visions in there? Was that supposed to be a joke, or did Eve really think people could see into the future with all the mirrors?

As she moved around in a little circle, the flame cast shadows all around. She could imagine going crazy in that room. That had to be how people saw visions. Was she supposed to stay in long enough to go insane and see visions? Of what—her future? A vision of how to escape would be nice, but that wasn't going to happen.

She stopped moving and stared at the reflections—which were a lot with the mirrors playing off each other. Even though she wasn't moving any longer, some of the images appeared to be. Was it because of the flickering flame or the reflections going on into infinity?

Or was she losing her mind already? Was it supposed to work that fast? No, it was probably because Chester had been working on her. She'd been locked in the barn cellar, dealt with Chester's threats and his locking her in Heather's room. Not to mention forcing her to cut and color her hair and everything else he had done.

She never knew what to expect because when he seemed to relax, a blowup wasn't far off.

Macy was almost jealous of Heather. She'd been able to get away from him. But where was she now? The last diary entry Macy had read, Heather was about to be taken away to a mental institute, removing Chester of his parental rights.

It was too bad they hadn't taken things a step farther and locked him up. They must not have found any proof of him killing his wife. Heather had been certain something horrible had happened to her mom, but no one would listen to her.

Chester knew how to get what he wanted, so it was no surprise that he had found a way to avoid being discovered having anything to do with whatever had happened to Karla.

As Macy stared into one mirror, she swore she saw the image of someone else join the hundreds of her in it. She jumped in surprise. She looked around the room, spinning in a circle. Her skin crawled. She was alone.

It had to have been her mind playing tricks on her. Maybe thinking about Chester wasn't the best thing to do while in the creepy room. She tried to stare at the floor, away from the trillions of images of her, but she couldn't. Her eyes pulled her to look up. Part of her was drawn to the images.

The reflections jumped as the flame flickered from her spinning around moments ago. She was adjusting to the many images, not finding them so creepy. She stared into her own eyes in one particularly large mirror. There seemed to be an infinite number of her.

It was actually kind of interesting. Looking at so many of her, trailing back like a slinky. A human slinky. But not just one. Due to all of the mirrors, there were countless reflections of her slinky-self from various angles.

She stared at the image directly in front of her. It narrowed its eyes as Macy did. It moved the candle up when she did. It scratched her nose when she did. Then it smiled.

Macy froze. She was sure she hadn't smiled. Not only that, but she felt like she was being watched. Of course she was being watched. She stared at the one that had smiled, waiting to see if it would do anything else.

Her mind had to be playing tricks on her. That was the only explanation. There was no way her reflection could smile on its own. Why hadn't she paid closer attention to the other images? Then she would know if any of them had smiled or if it had been just the one.

Of course it had only been the one she had been staring at. It only smiled because it was in her imagination. It was no wonder they had houses of mirrors at carnivals.

Did Jonah and Eve routinely send people there as a punishment? But Eve had acted as though it was an honor to go in. Macy would have to ask Luke about it later. Or what if she brought it up and no one knew about the mirrored room? They would think that she was crazy.

Her reflection winked at her. Macy stared, holding tighter to the candle, which shook. The wink had to have been from the flicker of the flame. Obviously her reflection hadn't winked at her any more than it had smiled.

Could she leave the house of horrors yet? Eve wouldn't send her back in, would she? Macy needed to get out before her mind *really* started playing tricks on her.

She took a deep breath and made her way back to the door. Macy turned the knob, but it wouldn't budge. Her stomach twisted in knots.

Macy twisted the knob again, this time making noise. If Eve was still out there, she would let Macy out. Wouldn't she? She would have to, right?

She looked around for a place to set the candle, but it didn't have a holder so it would roll to the ground, no matter what she did. She couldn't risk the flame going out.

Accidentally looking up, Macy saw the little flame in a mirror. As it moved back and forth, it became larger with each movement until it took up the entire mirror. None of the other mirrors showed the enlarged flame, but the one that had grown covered Macy completely. She blinked fast to get the image to return to normal, but it didn't.

She shook her head, finding that the blaze had grown even more. Macy saw herself, but not as she really was. The image of her walked out of the flame, looked around, and then ran. She looked terror stricken as she ran, the fire chasing after her.

Macy looked away and pulled on the knob, twisting at the same time. "I'm ready to get out!" She kept that up for a couple minutes, before giving up.

Had Eve gone back to Chester and the prophets? Were they all laughing at her? Maybe they were all standing outside the door, enjoying themselves.

"Let me out!" She banged on the door with her free hand. "I'm done!" No response.

She tried the knob one last time and then leaned against the door, sliding to the floor. She looked around, still seeing too many images of herself. Soon she would see visions, but not because she was some kind of seer. Because she was going crazy.

Every time she thought things couldn't get any worse, they always found a way to do exactly that. She didn't even want to wonder what could top the mirror room. She looked at her feet, refusing to acknowledge the mirrors. They could force her to be in there, but they couldn't make her look at the reflections.

It was the one thing she could actually control, and she knew that focusing on that would be what would keep her going until she was finally presented with a way to escape—even if was years down the road.

She would let them think they could control her, but they would never control her thoughts. They couldn't get in there, and as far as Macy was concerned, they never would. Let them think she was stupid enough to believe their insanity. It was to her advantage. The moment she allowed them in, that was when she would lose.

As long as she held onto reality, she stood a chance at getting back home. It was a small chance at this point, but at least it was something. It was more than just something—it was all she had.

Light from the candle shone on the floor, light also bouncing from the mirrors.

"Chester is not my dad. These people are not prophets." She repeated that until she grew tired of whispering. If anything, repeating it would reinforce reality so that they couldn't get in. She had to make sure that her defenses were stronger than their tactics to bring her down.

Sure, no one other than Chester knew the truth—that she wasn't Heather—but that didn't change the fact that they all wanted her to become an obedient member of the community. She couldn't put her finger on it, but for some reason, she couldn't help thinking that Luke wanted out too. Maybe it was the mirrors getting to her.

Even if she was wrong about him, there had to be others. Or at least *an* other. Surely, she wasn't the only one dragged into this place against her will, wanting to go back to texting and posting status updates. She missed taking selfies and even bickering with Alex.

While Macy sat surrounded by mirrors in the middle of a community of crazy people, was her family thinking about her too? Did they buy Chester's fake updates that she had run away? Were they mad at her? Did they have an inkling that she had been taken against her will?

Did Zoey know enough about "Jared" to figure it out? They were best friends and Macy told her everything. Zoey would know that something was wrong. She would know the status updates were fake. But would anyone listen to her?

Macy leaned her head against the door. The community would be the last place anyone would look for her.

The doorknob jingled above her. Macy jumped up before it would open and send her falling to the ground.

Surprise

ZOEY SAT IN front of her plate, pushing the food around. She had no appetite, and just looking at it made her sick. Was it because of being pregnant, the news of the body, or withdrawals from smoking?

"Aren't you going to eat?" her mom asked.

"How can you expect me to eat at a time like this?" Zoey snapped, and then glared at her.

"Don't look at me like that. You're the one supporting another life."

"I'm not hungry. If I really needed to eat, the food wouldn't turn my stomach."

"You can't think about only yourself anymore. That's what's going to happen if you decide to keep it. Nothing is going to be about you again. Every decision you make has to be in the baby's best interest."

Zoey bit her tongue, wanting to tell her mom that she'd already given up cigarettes, and the headaches were killing her. "You think I don't know that?"

"You need to eat."

"I'm not hungry!" Zoey slammed the fork down. "I'm going to puke if I eat. Why can't you have some understanding? Do you even know what it means that they found a body? It could belong to my best friend."

Valerie's face softened. "You know I'm worried about you."

"Do I?" Zoey's eyebrows came together.

"Of course I'm worried, Zo. I wish I could do something to fix the whole situation with Macy. I would love nothing more than to flip a switch and make it so that she never disappeared."

"I've hardly seen you shed a tear."

"I'm being strong for you. Not only that, but I have to take care of our family financially. You know that. I've cried over Macy's disappearance, but I don't have room to wallow. I have to take care of you. That's part of being a parent—a single parent, in particular. I can't rely on someone else to help out. It's all on me or we lose the house and other nice things we've gotten used to."

Zoey shook her head. "You could try showing a little empathy, you know. Just a little would be nice."

"Empathy? You think I haven't shown you any?"

"Not really, no."

"This is getting us nowhere. If you're not hungry, then go upstairs and get some rest. You need to take care of yourself."

"Whatever." Zoey threw her napkin onto the plate, stormed to her room and slammed the door.

Her headache roared in protest. When would that stop? The pain would go away as soon as her body figured out that she wasn't going to smoke anymore, right? She didn't bother turning on the light, enjoying the darkness of the room.

She got comfortable on her bed. She probably could have slept for a week if her mom would let her.

The cell phone's light was blinking. She grabbed it out of her bag and scrolled through a long list of texts. Tons of people were asking if she was okay and giving their condolences.

Macy wasn't dead! Couldn't they get that? *A body had been found.* Why assume that it was Macy?

She dropped her phone on the ground, not wanting to read any more texts. She wasn't going to shed another tear over that body until she found out it was Macy. No one who had known her had even seen the body—the cops wouldn't even let them look at it because it was in bad shape, whatever that meant.

Zoey's eyelids grew heavier by the second, and she gave into them, slinking down further under her covers. Sleep was most welcome, especially if it got her away from her headache and overall soreness.

Something woke her up, but she didn't know what. She sat up, looking around. A little light was coming through her blinds, but she didn't feel like she had gotten any sleep.

She heard a noise.

What was that? Is that what had woken her?

Heart pounding, she looked around the room, not seeing anything out of place. She pulled her hair back behind her shoulder. She had heard something; she was sure of that much.

Zoey grabbed the baseball bat she kept by her bed at her mom's insistence and crept out of bed. She tip-toed to her door, listening.

Everything was quiet. Zoey grabbed the door knob and turned it slowly, holding her breath.

The hallway was dark, having no windows to give any light. She looked down the hall, still not hearing anything. Standing still, she waited, clutching the bat. If she heard anything, she would swing. No questions asked.

There was the noise again down the hall to the right, near her mom's room. It sounded like a thump. She tip-toed in the direction, being as quiet as she could be, careful not to bump against the wall even though she stayed close to it.

Zoey stopped in front of her mom's door, listening. She heard the thump again. She couldn't tell what it was, but her mom could be in danger.

She heard something slide across the floor. The image of someone dragging her mom made her blood run cold. She threw open the door, ready to attack.

Her mom turned, looking frightened. "Zoey! What on earth?" She had a phone up to her ear. "I'm going to have to call you back." She closed the phone and set it on her dresser. "Are you all right, honey?"

Zoey lowered the bat. "What was all that noise? You scared the crap out of me."

"I'm sorry. I wasn't expecting you up this early. Are you okay?"

"Now I am, I guess. I thought I heard an intruder."

Sadness washed over Valerie's face. "We really need to get you into see a psychologist, dear. With everything you've been through, you're under a lot of stress. Do you remember I upgraded our security system after the Mercer's house was broken into? Not only that, there's always a cop across the street watching their house. If anything strange happened here, they would be right over."

"Who were you talking to?"

"Don't worry about it. Are you—?"

"Of course I'm going to worry about it. What time is it? Who would you be on the phone with this early? Grandma's not sick again, is she?"

"No, she's fine."

"What, then?"

"Zoey, there are some things that kids don't need to worry about."

"Kid? I'm no kid. I'm a teenager, Mom. I'm old enough to have a baby, because, oh, I *am* having one. After scaring the crap out of me, I think I deserve to know."

"I didn't mean to scare you. I'm sorry. I was just rearranging some of the furniture in here. It was bad timing, my nerves are shot these days too."

"Why don't you want to tell me who that was?"

A strange look came over her face, and then she patted her messy bed. "Have a seat, Zo."

Zoey sat, shaking her head in disbelief. "Let's hear it."

Her mom sat next to her, patting the top of Zoey's hand. "I don't want to put more on your plate, but you deserve the truth."

"What is it?" Zoey's stomach dropped to the floor and dread washed over her.

Her mom looked into her eyes. "That was your dad."

The room spun. "What? How did you...? I mean, what? How did you find him?"

"Ever since you told us about the pregnancy, I've been searching. It's obvious you're crying out for help. You need both of your parents, and that's one thing I can't give you by myself."

"I don't understand."

"I'm trying to get him to come back here. He needed the same speech I gave you about putting his child first."

Zoey clenched her fists. "I don't need him. He's never been here. He has no right to tell me what to do. He took off without a word, never once doing anything to take care of me."

Valerie frowned. "I wouldn't say never."

"What do you mean?" Zoey stood up. "All he's done is provide DNA. That's it. Because he's Japanese, everyone thinks you adopted me. Just tell him to stay there. We don't need him."

"That's the problem. We do. You need your dad, Zo, and I should have had this talk with him long ago. Maybe you wouldn't be in this mess." She looked at Zoey's stomach.

"And you think bringing my dad into this is going to help? He doesn't know anything about me."

"I know. You two need to get to know each other."

"What's that going to help?"

"It's obvious that you need him in your life."

"Ugh! You keep saying that. We've done just fine without him."

"Just fine? You call this *just fine*?"

"Do you know how many girls get pregnant? It was probably different way back when you were in high school."

Valerie laughed. "It wasn't that long ago, Zo."

"Yeah, it was. Things were so different. Could girls get an abortion without their parents knowing?"

"I honestly wouldn't even know. I had a nurse try to talk me into the pill when I was a little older than you, but I wasn't interested. My focus was getting into college. All I wanted was to get the career that I now have."

"Well, whatever it used to be like, now some girls don't even bother with the pill. If the guy doesn't have his own protection, they just get the morning after pill or have an abortion. It pretty much happens all the time."

"Back to the topic. I want your dad to move over here."

"Don't bother. I'm sure he's happy with his own family."

"No, he doesn't have a family."

Zoey raised an eyebrow.

"He plays baseball over there. He always dreamed of playing, but couldn't even make the minors here, so he went back home to play."

"A sport is more important than me? What a tool."

"It's not like that." Valerie sighed.

"What's it like, then?"

"I didn't want to hold him back when I got pregnant. Neither of us were looking for a long-term relationship. We were just having a little fun. We met through some mutual friends one summer. I'm a strong woman and figured I could handle raising you on my own." She smiled. "I even thought it would be easier because then I wouldn't have to argue with him on how to raise you."

"That doesn't change the fact that he walked away."

"He hasn't forgotten about you. On a pretty regular basis, I receive 'anonymous' deposits in my account. He thinks it's important to support you. Since I don't need his money, I've been keeping it for you in a savings account. You have a nice amount built up for college."

"And you never once thought to mention this to me? Here I've been thinking that he doesn't care." Zoey crossed her arms. "You could have called him any time you wanted?"

Valerie shook her head. "It took me some time to find him. Like I said, he left anonymous deposits. I still don't have his address or anything. I managed to find an email address and then he agreed to talk with me on the phone. He was actually benched with an injury since last season. They're talking about letting him retire since it looks like he can't play this season either, so this might be the perfect time for him to return."

"I don't want him in my life!" Zoey ran out of the room before her mom could see the tears.

Discussion

THE WALK TO school was an uncomfortable silence. Macy wanted to talk to Rebekah, but was afraid. Rebekah had barely made eye contact with Macy since Chester's outburst. Rebekah had been jumpy around both Macy and Chester.

Macy was still shaken from the whole vision room thing. She wasn't sure how she'd made it through the rest of the day. She hadn't been able to stop thinking about the mirrors—especially the images that appeared to change. Chills ran through her each time she thought about it. It had to have been her mind playing tricks on her. Or maybe it was the flickering light from the small candle.

It also didn't help that Eve had had a thousand questions about the experience, none that Macy had wanted to answer. She wasn't sure what Eve wanted to hear. Macy would have said anything—anything at all—to avoid ever having to go back in there again.

She had ended up admitting to having seen a couple things, and much to her relief, Eve hadn't pressed. Her smile had been wide; she had been thrilled that the daughter of the up and coming prophet had seen a vision. She told Macy that visions were private and needed to be kept to oneself until the right time.

"Are you okay?" Rebekah asked, bringing her back to the present.

"Yeah."

"No, I mean it, Heather. The way that your dad's been acting…I just want to make sure you're okay."

"I'm fine."

Rebekah came closer and spoke softer. "Does he act like that a lot, or he just stressed about training to become a prophet? You can talk to me."

If Macy said anything, would Rebekah tell Chester? Macy had to be careful with her wording. "He can be...a little moody. Don't tell him I said anything."

"Of course. I was shocked when he reacted like that. You looked more concerned than surprised, so I thought that wasn't the first time. Are there certain things that tend to set him off?"

Macy's heart raced. "I don't really know."

Rebekah gave her an inquisitive look.

Did she know that Macy was holding back?

"I don't want you to fear me, Heather. Yes, my first responsibility is to my husband, but as your new mother, I also have an enormous responsibility to take care of you."

That answered that. Chester came first, and if he ever pressed Rebekah to find out what Macy had told her in private, she'd talk. "Thanks," Macy said.

"I still want to tell you about my life before I joined the community. It sounded like you were interested, but that will have to wait. I do hope we can be friends." Rebekah smiled.

Macy nodded. "That would be nice."

"As far as today, please stay inside the schoolroom. I won't tell your dad if you talk to boys, but please—please—don't go anywhere with one. Luke is a trustworthy young man, and you would do well to become friends with him, but please also make friends with some of the girls. We don't want to upset your dad again."

"Okay."

They turned a corner and the school was in sight. Rebekah took Macy's hand and gave a squeeze. "Everything is going to be all right. If we work together, we'll figure out how your dad ticks and we'll learn to live in such a way as to not incite his anger again. Sound good?"

Macy had to stop herself from laughing. Good luck with that. "Sure." She hoped that Rebekah didn't pick up on her sarcasm.

"If your hand cramps up—and it might until you adjust—let me know. I'll have you do some reading or have one of the girls sit with you and go over some of what you need to learn."

They entered the schoolroom without a word. Everyone sat at their desks doing their work. Macy sat next to Luke.

He looked up at her. "I missed you yesterday afternoon."

"Something came up."

"I see." Luke held each her gaze for a moment and then went back to his papers.

She opened the book in front of her, getting ready to copy from it. She'd have to write slowly so that hopefully her hand wouldn't cramp. Why bother writing fast anyway? Was there a rush to learn this stuff? Of course not. What she needed was to find a way out of the community.

Even if she could get out, did they have the woods booby trapped? What about wild animals? How would she get home? Hitchhike? Then she would risk running into another Chester—or even someone worse. Macy shuddered.

"You all right?"

Macy looked over at Luke. "Yeah." She picked up the pencil and copied from where she had left off the day before. She wanted to talk to Luke, but how?

She sat in silence writing for what felt like hours. Maybe it was. It wasn't like there was a clock on the wall. They wouldn't want to use that evil electricity.

At least her hand felt okay. She was treating it like a wounded bird, careful not to let it cramp again.

A tapping noise in the front of the room grabbed Macy's attention. Rebekah stood in the front of the room, tapping on the chalk board. "It's time to stretch our legs and take a break. We'll reconvene in ten minutes."

Luke looked at Macy. "Want some fresh air?"

Her eyes widened. Could they, without her getting into trouble? She noticed some of the other kids going outside. If she talked to some of them she should be okay talking with Luke also. "Sure."

"It's all overwhelming, isn't it?" Luke gave her a reassuring smile.

"You have no idea." Why had she said that? Her mouth seemed to run on its own when talking to him.

His eyebrow arched, but didn't say anything. He held his hand out, indicating for her to go first and she headed for the door. When they got outside, the cold air felt good and the sun shining down felt even better.

She stood off to the side, watching the kids talk.

Aside from the white clothes and the buns on the girls, they all seemed like normal teenagers. Except that they weren't goofing off or picking on each other. She wasn't sure if she missed the kids running around acting like caged animals.

She kind of liked the serenity of the community—not that she wanted to become one of them. Maybe she was just glad to be away from Chester. It had been torture spending so much time with him since he'd taken her from her family. At least here, she had school and Chester spent a lot of time with the prophets, but he made sure to drive Macy crazy when they were home.

"Care to share your thoughts?" Luke asked.

Macy shrugged. "Just taking everything in. It's a big change."

"It usually is. Some kids have a really hard time getting used to this way of life."

Something about the tone of his voice told her he wasn't referring to hand cramps. "What do you mean?"

"I've seen people have breakdowns or tantrums because it's too much of a change for them."

"Then what?"

"Sometimes they have to stay away from school for a while until they're able to come back and behave properly. Other times, they have to be shamed. It depends on what they do."

"What did you think when I didn't come back yesterday afternoon?"

"I hoped for the best since Teacher didn't say anything. You hadn't done anything wrong. Your hand just cramped up. I assumed that you were resting or studying at home."

"Something like that."

"Is your hand okay now?" Luke asked.

Macy held it up. "A little sore, but otherwise it's fine."

Luke reached for it and rubbed. Her heart raced. She loved the feel of his skin against hers, but what if word got back to Chester?

She closed her eyes. Whatever Chester did to her would be worth it. An adorable boy cared enough to hold and rub her tired hand. He couldn't take that away from her, even if she did get punished.

Luke's fingers slid down to her wrist under her sleeve again. Macy's eyes popped open. Luke smiled at her and then hid their hands behind his back. Macy stared into his eyes, feeling her face flush. He rubbed his fingers back and forth along her arm just above her wrist.

She opened her mouth to say something, but nothing came. Her skin tingled where his fingers touched her arm.

Luke slid his hand back down to hers, and then squeezed. He cleared his throat. "Perhaps I should introduce you to the others?" Luke asked.

"Yeah, sure." Macy shook her head, trying to clear it. "That's probably a good idea."

"Maybe." The skin around his eyes wrinkled a little as he grinned.

Macy's pulse quickened. He was adorable, and he wasn't repulsed by her.

"Come on," Luke said.

He walked to one of the groups and introduced them to her. She tried to remember their names, but they all had strange names. They all stared at her, not saying anything. Were they expecting her to say something? If so, what?

"It was nice to meet you all." She went back to where she had been standing with Luke, and the girls went back to their conversation.

Luke joined her.

"That went well," Macy joked.

"I think they're intimidated by you."

Macy laughed. He had to be kidding. "By me? Why?"

"You're the daughter of Jonah's new favorite. Everyone has been talking about your dad since before you guys arrived. Jonah isn't one to keep his visions to himself. He spends hours in the vision room and as I'm sure you've noticed in the nightly meetings, he loves sharing every single detail."

"Yeah. I've noticed."

Luke looked like was trying to cover a laugh. Macy thought it was cute the way he fought to keep his composure.

"Jonah received visions long before he met your dad. He left the community for a while, following clues from his visions until he found him. Did your dad tell you how excited he was to find out that he had been chosen?"

"He's mentioned it."

Luke raked his fingers through his hair. Macy watched each strand fall back into place. It looked so soft she wanted to touch it. His hair was a nice, sandy color. It had speckles of brown and blonde strands all throughout. She moved her gaze down to his eyes. Macy had never seen such kind eyes before. Or was it just because she was used to Chester and his frightening stares?

Either way, Luke held a genuine graciousness about him. His eyes lit up when he smiled, and his voice was soothing. That's when Macy realized that he'd been talking to her, but she hadn't heard a word of it.

"Don't you think?" Luke asked.

Macy's cheeks burned. "What?"

Luke gave her an amused look. Her stomach twisted in knots.

"How much did you miss? I said that Jonah wanted to return with your dad as soon as he found him, but your dad wasn't going to leave the world without you, so we had to wait."

Instead of replying, Macy looked up at the sky. A cloud reminded her of a sleeping cat. Macy and Zoey had spent countless afternoons finding shapes in clouds, and even going as far as creating elaborate stories to go with them.

A lump formed in her throat. Would she ever see Zoey again, or would she live out the rest of her days in the community? Worse, would she one day succumb to it?

Macy blinked away tears. Images of her being part of Jonah's inner circle flooded her mind. She would never let that happen. She was Macy Mercer, not Heather Woodran. Chester was not her dad. The community was not her home.

She looked over at Luke and saw him looking at her, his eyes full of concern.

"Are you upset, Heather? Do you want to talk?"

Her heart sunk at him calling her Heather. She looked deep into his light brown eyes. Could she trust him? She wanted to believe she could, but the truth was that she didn't know who she could trust.

"How did you end up here?" Macy asked. "In the community, I

mean."

"We were down on our luck, and Jonah met my mom. My dad died and we were about to lose our house."

Macy gasped. "I'm so sorry. That's horrible."

"Thanks. It was a long time ago. Anyway, my mom's job was already on the line because she couldn't focus after losing my dad. Not only that, but she was dealing with me and my anger. She was waiting for an appointment to learn about state housing when Jonah approached her. The rest, as they say, is history."

"Is that what happens usually? Jonah goes out and finds people who are having a rough time?"

"Sometimes. He likes to find people who need hope. People like my mom. It's not the people living the high life who are looking for hope."

Macy studied his face again. "Are you glad to be here?" she asked.

"I'm grateful to be off the streets. Mom says that's where we were headed. She might have lost me otherwise. Who knows where I would be if we weren't here? And at least I'm still with her."

Macy felt like she could trust him—and she had to tell someone that she really wasn't Chester's daughter. Her heart pounded nearly out of her chest as she decided to open up to him.

She opened her mouth to say something, but Rebekah came out, announcing they needed to come back inside.

Revenge

ALEX ROLLED OVER, waking again. It was getting hard to tell the difference between dreams and reality. Was he really awake or was it just another dream? He pulled the blankets up over himself. He kept kicking them off despite being cold.

Weeks had passed since the body had been found. Alex wasn't sure how he had made it through them. He couldn't stop thinking about the body. Why did it take so long to get the results? They had sent it to Seattle because they were supposed to have more advanced equipment.

With three weeks, they should have been able to figure something out. What was wrong with them? Didn't they care? Or were they just stupid? The local cops had said that it might take months before they could get DNA results.

Why did it have to take so long? Three weeks was way too long to figure out if the body was his sister or not. How was he expected to wait even longer? Another month of this? He didn't want another hour of it.

Alex wanted answers, but on the other hand he wasn't sure. Did he really want to know if the body was Macy? What could be worse than losing his big sister? He hadn't even been able to say goodbye.

Alex pulled the pillow from under him and put it over his head trying to stop the tears that threatened.

Waiting sucked, and in this case, it really wasn't fair. Why couldn't they just have answers? They'd been waiting so long already.

It was enough to make him want to turn on the news or the computer, but he knew he would either end up depressed or angry. Some of the things he'd heard and read had really pissed him off. He knew he needed to avoid it now more than ever.

He rolled over again, keeping the pillow on top of him. What he needed was to think about something else. What else mattered, though? The things he used to enjoy only brought him more misery.

If he caught himself having fun, he was plagued with guilt, instantly remembering Macy. He shouldn't be having fun when she was probably out there somewhere not having any fun at all—or worse.

What would she think if she saw him? Would she think he was a jerk? Or would she be glad that he wasn't wallowing in pity?

A tear escaped, landing on his sheet. Why hadn't he been able to do anything to stop Macy? Had he pushed her away? She was always annoyed with his teasing. He knew that kids at school picked on her, even after losing her weight. Why had he been so insensitive?

Not that he was anywhere as mean as anyone at school, and he wasn't trying to be mean to her. He'd just been a normal brother. Brothers teased—even his dad told him that.

If he would have had any idea that she was going to disappear, whether running away or being kidnapped, he would have stopped. But there was nothing he could about that now.

Did she really know how he felt? She had to know how much he loved her. It wasn't like their entire relationship had been about him teasing her. They still talked and stuff, but obviously not enough.

This was getting him nowhere. Why couldn't he just sleep? Because his guilt wouldn't leave him alone even there. He should have been able to do something. What? He didn't know, but he could have done *something* to stop Macy from disappearing.

He closed his eyes tighter, trying to push the thoughts away. He focused on the black behind his eyes. He could feel more tears slipping out and all falling along the same path, pooling around his face.

He sat up. There was no way he could stay in bed. He couldn't stop thinking, and even if he could stop thinking about Macy, he would probably start thinking about Zoey and the baby, and he couldn't deal with that, either.

If Macy was dead, what would he do? How would he go on? Could he go on? Would he live with the guilt for the rest of his life? What would life be like? He didn't want to be an only child—he wasn't supposed to be. Macy was supposed to be there. They were *supposed* to bicker and bug each other. It was their job as siblings.

It was also his job to protect her. Even though he was younger, he was still her brother. He should have gone over to the high school and confronted those stupid jerks who were giving her a hard time.

He still could. It wasn't too late. *They* weren't missing. All of them were still at school, and Zoey knew them by name. He probably knew most of them too. *They* were the ones who had caused this. If they hadn't been so mean to her, Macy wouldn't have felt like she had to meet some guy online.

Alex had stopped working out after she disappeared, but it probably wouldn't take him long to get back into shape. He threw on a sweatshirt from the end of his bed and got up.

He went down to the garage to the punching bag and balled up his fists. He punched it. It felt good. He punched again. It felt even better. He imagined the faces of the jerks who had tormented his sister. He felt even better still.

Alex hit it until sweat poured down his face and back, and was breathing hard. He felt great. He would have to remember to use it daily. Taking deep breaths, he found that he had more energy. He went to his dad's weights and grabbed some dumbbells—the ones he was sure he had used last and did reps.

The muscles burned in a good way. He was doing what he needed and once he got himself back into shape, he was going to confront every person who had made fun of Macy. He didn't care that he wasn't supposed to hit girls—those ones had it coming.

He grabbed a different set of dumbbells and did some squats. He had to strengthen everything. It shouldn't take him long to get back to where he was. He'd only missed a month; it wasn't like he'd stopped for a year.

He grunted his way through the last set and put everything back in place. Not that his dad would notice anything had been moved out of place. He'd also stopped working out.

Alex went back to his room, allowing himself to enjoy the burn of his muscles. He felt powerful and he would face the ones responsible for pushing his sister away. Even if he didn't lay a hand on them—and how he wanted to rearrange their butt-ugly faces—he would at least know that he *could*.

Someone needed to stand up for Macy, and he was going to do it. Better late than never, as his dad always said. Those girls needed to pay, and they would. They probably thought they'd gotten away with it, but they were wrong.

In fact, he would find a way to make them pay in ways that would hurt worse than a good beating. They'd hurt Macy emotionally. Those horrible excuses for humans had nearly destroyed his sister.

He could still see the pain in Macy's eyes, which he'd pretty much ignored at the time. He felt bad, but instead of asking what he could do, he did what any twelve-year-old boy would do. He teased her. He thought if he could just get her mind off what the kids had been saying, she would forget about it.

Obviously, he hadn't understood just how much it had hurt her—or the lengths she would go to because of it. Going vegan was pretty extreme. Meeting a guy online, that wasn't so strange. But meeting him alone at night, that was pretty crazy. Even he knew that much.

He went to Macy's room. Hopefully she still hid her diaries in the same places she used to. He went to her bed and pulled back the mattress and felt for the loose fabric. When he did, he pulled it back and dug his hand around until he felt the diary. If Macy hadn't had such good hiding spots, the police would have found and taken them.

Alex pulled the diary and looked at it. He didn't recognize that one, so it had to have been new. At least newer. He hadn't read her diaries in a long time. He pulled it out and looked around for one of her hair clips. The clip was perfect for picking the lock—they always were.

He skimmed through the first pages; mostly she was griping about school. Then the whole tone changed when Snowflake, the family cat, died. Macy had loved him the most, always calling him a beautiful baby. Apparently, she had been so upset about it that her grades slipped.

Then the entries got even darker when she talked about the kids calling her "Muffin Top Macy," and she couldn't even eat lunch in the cafeteria without people mooing at her. Alex balled up his fist again, taking note of the names mentioned.

This was the type of crap that kids killed themselves over.

Those losers would pay—they would pay dearly. Alex would see to that.

He took the diary back to his room. Where had he put his phone? He dug around his messes until he finally found it.

Alex got the camera ready, he opened the diary to the pages about the girls at school and took pictures of the entries. Then uploaded them to his profile. He set them to public so the world could see.

Having the pictures was proof that Macy had written them. No one could argue.

Then he wrote a little intro to each picture, tagging as many of the girls as he could. He was "friends" with most of them, making it easy. Fury ran through him as he looked at the post button. With any luck, other kids would turn around and give them a taste of their own medicine. Those bitches were going to pay.

He pushed post.

Fretting

MACY'S MIND RACED as she did her copy work. She was all too aware of Luke sitting next to her. She kept sneaking peeks at him through the corner of her eyes. He was busy with his own work, appearing to be unaware of her.

The last three weeks she had tried to tell Luke the truth about her situation, but she had chickened out each time. In a way she was glad, because it gave her time to get to know him better—as well as she could only speak with him during their ten minute breaks twice a day.

Even though it wasn't a lot of time, it had been enough that she knew she could trust him. He wouldn't rat her out to Jonah or Chester. He wanted to help her, and even seemed to know that she wanted to tell him something.

Could things get worse if she told Luke that she'd been kidnapped? Maybe he would even help her.

But what if she was wrong about him? If Macy's desire to escape got into the wrong hands, she could get into trouble again. If she was publicly shamed, what letter would they pick? Would they give her B for blasphemy? Speaking out against Chester, who the almighty Jonah had received so many visions about? Or would it be an L for liar? They might just think she was making everything up about being kidnapped.

She sighed, louder than she had meant to.

Luke looked over at her, giving her a curious look. He was so cute Macy couldn't think of anything else when she looked at him.

Macy turned back to her papers and focused on her copy work, pretending he wasn't sitting there. The room felt like it was spinning out of control around her. Macy set her pencil down and took some deep breaths. White dots speckled her vision.

"Are you okay?" asked someone. Macy thought it might be Luke.

She tried to draw more deep breaths, but she couldn't get down far enough.

A hand rested on her shoulder. She looked up to see Rebekah. "Do you need air?"

Macy nodded.

"I'll go out with her," Luke said.

Alarm crossed over Rebekah's face. She pointed toward a girl and said something Macy couldn't understand.

Soon, she was standing outside with Luke and one of the girls he had introduced her to before.

Luke put his hand on Macy's shoulder and guided her to the side of the building. "Lean against the wall and put your head between your legs."

Macy looked at him like he was crazy.

"It'll help. Trust me."

Macy needed a sign. If she felt better after putting her head between her legs, then she would know she could tell Luke everything. Otherwise, if she didn't feel better, then it was a sign that he wasn't safe to talk to. She needed to stop being afraid of talking to him. He had done nothing other than be her friend for the last several weeks.

Macy positioned herself against the schoolhouse and bent over. She felt as ridiculous as could be, but hoped for an obvious sign.

"Stand up now. Slowly," Luke said.

Macy rose as slow as possible and looked around. The white dots were gone and her breathing came naturally. She had her answer. She would tell Luke everything as soon as possible.

"How do you feel?" he asked.

"Much better, actually."

"Do you want to stay out a bit longer?"

Macy nodded. She wanted to tell Luke about her being kidnapped right then, but didn't know anything about the girl. She looked her over at her. She had light brown hair and bright blue eyes. She looked nice enough, but then again so had Chester. Macy didn't know anything about the girl.

She gave Macy a look of concern. "Are you sure you're okay?"

"Yeah. I don't know what overcame me in there."

"I wouldn't worry about it. Everyone freaks out sometimes. It happens."

"What's your story?" Macy asked her.

"Like you, I was raised in the world. But then...well, life didn't exactly go the way I planned." She shrugged, looking away.

Luke looked at her. "Dorcas had a rough time transitioning to the lifestyle too."

"Dorcas? That must be rough." Where Macy was from, kids would have called her dork-us.

Dorcas smiled. "It's my Bible name."

"What's your real name?"

Dorcas and Luke exchanged a look. Luke turned to Macy. "We're not supposed to talk about our worldly names once we've received our new names."

"Of course. Sorry."

"What's your story?" Dorcas asked.

"Don't you know? Jonah found...my dad, and now here we are."

Dorcas looked around and stepped closer and lowered her voice. "Luke and I are trying to get out of here."

Macy's eyes widened. "What? Why are you telling me? I...I mean, I'm the daughter of Jonah's next prophet."

Luke stepped closer too. "There are a few of us who are working on it. I could tell by the look in your eyes at your unveiling that you didn't want to be here. I've been around long enough that it's easy to see who buys this stuff and who doesn't. After talking with you over the last few weeks, I know you want to leave also."

"But, you guys both have your new names. Doesn't that mean you've made your way through the ranks or something?" She turned to Luke. "The way you've been talking, it sounded like you believe everything they teach here."

"You're the daughter of Jonah's favorite. I had to feel you out even though I thought you wanted out too."

Dorcas nodded. "In case we can't find another way out, we're working our way up so that someday we'll be allowed to leave. You know, to look for new members. Only we won't come back."

Macy stared at them. Were they for real? "Wouldn't that take years?"

"More than likely," Dorcas said. "But at least it's better than nothing. I'd rather get out of here in ten years than never."

"I do want out too."

Luke and Dorcas exchanged a look.

"But I don't want to wait ten years," Macy said.

"Do you have a plan to get out sooner?" Luke asked.

"Well, no. But I want to come up with something. I need to get back to my family."

Dorcas tilted her head. "Chester isn't your family?"

"I...uh...well, it's complicated."

Luke stepped even closer. "Are you another kidnapped one?"

Macy's eyebrows came together. "How did you know? And what do you mean by another?"

"Are you really surprised that there are others like you?"

Macy shrugged.

"Trust me. You're far from the only one."

"Really?" Macy's stomach twisted in knots.

Dorcas nodded.

"Well, that gives us even more reason to break out of here. If there are others like me, we have to get them to their homes—their real homes."

Luke held up a hand. "Don't get anxious. One wrong move and we'll lose all chances of hope. We have to be meticulous and take everything at a snail's pace. It's fine to look for something else, but the best thing you can do is to try to move up the ranks, which means following the rules to a tee. Learn them, but don't internalize them."

"Isn't there a way to get out of the fence?" Macy asked.

"Have you looked at it?" Dorcas asked.

"What I mean," Macy said, "is that there has to be a weak spot. A loose board or something."

Dorcas shook her head. "There are people whose only job is to take care of the fence. They would spot something like that long before we did.

And besides, it would be most suspicious if we were examining the fence."

"But it has to be worth a try. We could come up with a good reason for looking at the fence."

Luke gave me a sad look. "Shortly after my mom and I joined, someone did try to get out. A kid who was probably about our age."

"What happened?" Macy asked. She held her breath.

"I never saw him again."

Macy looked back and forth between them. "What does that mean?"

"He disappeared. No one ever mentioned him, either."

"You mean…you think he died?" Macy whispered.

"Do you have a better explanation?"

Macy felt sick. They were as bad as Chester. Maybe worse.

Dorcas looked at her. "We have to think long-term, and you actually have the best chance of getting out with your dad working so closely with Jonah, Abraham and Isaac. Your dad could take you with him sometime."

"But then, what? I couldn't just run and save myself. The rest of you, I would have to get you out too."

Dorcas shook her head. "For one thing—"

The door opened and Rebekah came out, looking at Macy. "How are you feeling?"

"Better now. The fresh air must have been what I needed."

"Good. Now come back inside. We have plenty more to do before we take our lunch break. We don't want to find too few pages done when Eve checks the work, now do we?"

"No, Teacher," Dorcas and Luke said in unison.

They went inside, but Macy couldn't focus. Luke and Dorcas actually wanted out, and not only that, but other kids in the same room as her had also been kidnapped.

The community was the perfect place for a criminal to go. Had the whole thing been masterminded by one? Was Jonah a mass murderer? Or was he just power hungry, and it was only a coincidence that the community was the perfect getaway for someone who needed to hide?

Luke nudged her with his elbow. "At least *pretend* to do your work." He winked at her.

"Right." Macy picked up her pencil and looked at the book. She wrote a few sentences and then looked around the room. Who else in there was heartbroken because they'd been stolen from their families?

Macy felt something on her foot. She looked down and saw Luke's foot on top of hers. He moved it over so that it was next to hers with their ankles touching because the fabric of their pants had risen.

She looked over at him, eyes wide. There was no way that was allowed.

"What?" he whispered, his voice dripping with innocence. As if he didn't know.

Macy elbowed him, but hoped he wouldn't move his foot. He didn't.

She looked around the room and made eye contact with Rebekah. Rebekah nodded down, indicating for Macy to get to work.

Would Macy really have to pretend to work her way up the ranks in order to get out? Luke and Dorcas had probably been around long enough to know that there wasn't another way out.

Something bumped her knee and she looked over at Luke. He gave her a knowing look and she got back to work. She would have to wait until later to process everything.

Macy was lucky enough to have three people on her side. Now all she needed was a plan. But Luke would have to move his foot before she could concentrate enough to think of anything.

Undoing

CHAD GOT OUT of bed, careful not to wake Alyssa. She'd been awake half the night crying. So had he, actually. He hoped to God that the body didn't belong to Macy. If he thought about it, he knew that he would immediately start processing the emotions of it all, and he couldn't go there. Not unless he knew for sure.

Until he had proof of anything else, he was operating under the assumption that his daughter was safe somewhere. Where? Only she knew that, but he had to hold onto the hope. He wasn't giving up yet.

Since he couldn't sleep, he needed to get on his blog to publish the letters to Macy. In just the previous afternoon, the idea had exploded. Nearly everyone wanted to write their letter. He was going to end up with an entire series of posts rather than just one. Alyssa's parents wanted to write one, as did other relatives and some friends from school that Zoey had contacted.

Chad went to his office and sat down. He saw yesterday's coffee still sitting there. He looked at it, tempted. It was probably less than twelve hours old. He picked it up and drank. It tasted just as good as it had the day before, only cold. The caffeine gave him a jolt of energy and that was all he needed, anyway.

Taking another sip, he turned his laptop on. He opened the browser and it went to his profile, the last page he had opened. Chad almost typed in the address for his blog when he noticed an unusually high number of notifications. Fifty-six? He didn't even get that many when he took a weekend off.

His stomach twisted. Whatever it was, it couldn't be good. Had people been tagging him with more theories about the body? If that was the case, he would be unfriending and blocking each one of them, no matter who they were.

He scanned through the list of notifications, trying to make sense of them. There appeared to be some handwritten notes everyone was commenting on. He narrowed his eyes and nearly threw up all over his keyboard when he realized he was looking at Macy's handwriting.

Did someone find a note she left somewhere? Chad clicked on one of the images of the notes and noticed the date. It was nearly a year old.

He read it, feeling even worse. Had her friends actually said those things to her? Why hadn't she told him? He would have gone to the school and had it out with that wimp of a principal. Then he would have found the parents of those girls and given them a piece of his mind. No one talked about his daughter that way. No one.

He read through the comments left on the pictures of the notes, trying to catch up. Hundreds of people had left comments. Who had posted the pictures, anyway? He looked up and saw Alex's profile photo. He looked at the time of the post and read what Alex wrote.

Chad shook his head as he read through the rest of the comments. People were saying horrible things about the girls Macy had written about. People were arguing. Some were even using all-caps and swear words Chad had never heard before.

He clicked Alex's profile and saw several more pictures. Scrolling down, he saw there were even more. What had Alex done? Each one had over hundreds of comments each.

His head spun at the thought of trying to catch up. As he stared at the screen, new comments showed up faster than he could hope to keep up with.

What had Alex been thinking?

Posting those diary entries hadn't been the wisest of moves. Especially tagging the girls mentioned in them. The backlash could get ugly. From the looks of the comments, it already had.

Chad leaned back in his chair, scanning over the comments. Damage control. He had to think fast.

His head was spinning, so he got up and went to Alex's room. He opened the door to find Alex wrapped around his blankets. One bare leg was sticking out and Alex's head was hanging off the side of the bed. He was snoring.

Heart softening, Chad went over and moved Alex over to his pillow, fixing his blankets. How long had he been awake, reading Macy's diaries? How much time had he spent stewing over them?

Chad stood there, listening to Alex breathe. He hadn't done that since the kids were little. His heart ached, wishing he could run down the hall and check on his little girl. Blinking back tears, he leaned over and kissed Alex on the forehead.

He had mixed feelings about Alex posting the diary entries, especially since Chad was the one who would have to do damage control, but he couldn't be mad at Alex for standing up for his sister. When things calmed down, he would have to talk with him about discretion.

He couldn't blame Alex though. Those kids at school had been horrible. What else had Macy gone through? Those entries had to only be a snippet of the whole picture. Chad scanned the messy, darkened room for the diary, but couldn't find anything.

Chad sat in Alex's chair. Why hadn't he spent more time trying to figure out *why* Macy had done the things she had done? If he had asked her why she had wanted to go vegan, would she have opened up to him? Could he have helped her? Would she have avoided looking for love on the internet?

If he would have had any inkling of what she had been going through, things might have turned out differently. He knew it was useless looking back, thinking of what he could have done to change things. There was no going back.

He would have been a better dad—to both of them. And a better husband for that matter. But he couldn't do anything about that now. When Alex got up, he would ask him questions, and even more importantly, he would listen, really listen.

Looking over at Alex, he knew that would be a while. The kid had probably been up half the night, reading and posting. At least he was home, safe and sound. He was where they could take care of him.

Chad's heart swelled, watching his son sleep. At least he had a second chance. He hoped to God he would be given a second chance with Macy, but either way, he was going to turn things around for Alex.

He would be a completely different dad from here on out.

Listening to the soft, rhythmic breathing, Chad felt himself getting sleepy. His eyelids grew heavy, and he didn't bother fighting them. He turned to the side in the over-sized chair and allowed himself to get some sleep too.

He felt hands on his shoulder, waking him. He blinked a few times, looking around. The room was bright like late morning. Alyssa stood in front of him, the light shining around her as if she was an angel.

"Is everything okay?" she asked. "Why are you sleeping here?"

Nothing would be okay until Macy came back, but at least he had the rest of his family and he had the chance to be a new man for them. He grabbed her and wrapped her in a tight hug.

She seemed surprised at first, but then put her arms around him too. "What's going on?"

Chad looked over at Alex, still sleeping. He put his finger over his mouth and pointed toward the door, indicating that they should talk somewhere else.

Alyssa nodded and then he stood and stretched. He took her hand and led her out of the room, closing the door behind them.

She looked at him, her eyes filled with worry. "Is Alex okay? Why were you sleeping in there?"

"Let's get some coffee and talk in the kitchen."

"Okay." It sounded more like a question, but she went toward the stairs.

He took her hand and then she gave him a look he couldn't quite read. It was filled with too many emotions, which he fully understood. When they got to the kitchen, he asked if she was hungry.

"No. Just coffee's fine."

He poured the ground beans into the coffee maker, he told her about Alex's posts. By the time he sat down with the two steaming cups of coffee, he was telling her about the comments.

She just stared at him. "I hate social media. I really do. What are we going to do?"

"The good thing is that Alex is doing this because he loves Macy."

"Have you already talked to him about this? Is that why you were in there?"

He shook his head. "He was already sleeping when I got in there."

"Everyone has already seen those posts?"

"If you judge by the number of comments left, yes. Hundreds. Probably a lot more by now."

Alyssa put her face into her hands. "I don't know how much more of this I can take."

"I'll take care of it; you can feel free to stay away from the internet. Let's just focus on writing our letters to Macy."

She looked up at him. "Kids are going to be furious with Alex for posting that stuff. What if those girls turn on Alex too?"

"I don't think they'd dare. There were so many people commenting about being pissed at what they did to Macy. They're going to be the ones who need to worry."

"But if those girls get bullied due to what Alex posted, he could get into trouble."

"It's a good thing he stayed home from school today."

Done

MACY HELD THE pillow over her head, trying to ignore the sounds from Chester and Rebekah's room. It was too gross to think about. She had been trying not to listen to them for weeks. She had lost count of the days.

She distracted herself by thinking about Luke. Her cheeks warmed just picturing his face. He was so cute and he actually liked her, at least as a friend. If she was going to be stuck in the community, at least she would enjoy spending more time with him.

Would he tell her more? Luke really hadn't wanted to talk about an escape plan that morning. His gorgeous face had been stressed telling her about the kid who had gone missing.

The more she thought about him, the more surprised she was that he had taken an interest in her. He probably just saw her as the key to getting out of there since he was working on that himself. She would gladly spend as much time as needed with him. But because of Chester, she would probably have to make sure that Dorcas was with them at all times.

Chester had questioned both her and Rebekah about who Macy had spent time with. Rebekah had told him that she was making friends with Dorcas, but didn't mention anything about Luke. Macy said the same things, and Chester didn't have a tantrum. He hadn't returned to the nice guy he had been, but at least he hadn't locked her up or yelled at Rebekah.

Macy was tired. The nightly meetings always ran so late, and then they had to get up early for school. She moved the pillow from her head, but then was greeted with the sounds of a squeaking bed.

"Ugh!" She pulled it back over her ears, closing her eyes. She just wanted some sleep. She was certain that Chester had to be sleep depriving her on purpose. It was one way to keep her tired and less likely fight back if all she wanted to do was sleep.

Whatever she did, she needed to start acting like she wanted to be a part of things. Luke had been pretty sure that she would be able to go out of the walls with Chester at some point. If that was true, she needed to do what she could to make that happen sooner rather than later.

On the other hand, she needed find out if there was another way out. Who knew how long it would be before she was allowed to go out with Chester? She would probably have to pass whatever test it was to get her biblical name first. Most everyone seemed to have those. She hadn't met anyone yet with a non-Biblical name.

Macy lifted the pillow from her ear and immediately heard the sounds again. How much longer could they go? It wasn't the Olympics. She covered her ears. She had discovered that thinking about her family and life back home made her too sad, so she tried to think about something else.

Her mind wandered to Heather. Was she still in the mental facility, wasting away? What if no one believed her about her mom? The fact that Chester was walking around free proved that no one had found a body at least.

When she got out, she would have to figure out where Heather was. She would find the hospital and tell them everything if it meant getting Heather free. Hopefully that would also be enough to get Chester into jail. Even though there might be no proof about his wife, he would have to go to jail for kidnapping.

He couldn't claim insanity. It was definitely premeditated, the way that he had stalked her and pretended to be a teenager to lure her out there. If he didn't go to jail, then maybe Heather was safer wherever she was.

As she thought about it, Macy finally drifted off to sleep.

She had dreams of climbing over the fence and getting cut on the wiring only to fall to the ground on the other side and end up attacked by wild animals with sharp teeth and ugly faces.

Macy sat up in a cold sweat, gasping for air. She looked around the room, taking a minute to figure out where she was. Her hair was a jumbled mess around her face and she clawed at it, getting it out of her way. Holding it between her fingers, she stared at the light color and shorter length Chester had forced her into.

The only good thing about her hair was that it was going to have dark roots soon, if she didn't already. There weren't mirrors available, she couldn't know for sure. Once Macy did have obvious roots, Chester would have to explain her hair to everyone. Or did it even matter? No one in the community knew what Heather looked like, so it probably didn't matter. And even if it did, he would have figured something out. He had everything planned out perfectly.

Anger and hate ran through her. Not only did he take her away from her family, but he had stripped her identity too. She moved her hand, looking at her hair in different angles, allowing the hate and rage to build.

She was *done*. Done being nice. Done pretending to be Heather. Done living in fear. It was over. She was going to find a way out if it killed her—and it very well might. She had spent enough time playing it safe. Where had it gotten her? Nowhere. She was still no closer to her family. In fact, she was probably farther away than ever.

They were probably worried sick. What if they thought she was dead? Chester would love nothing more. Then he wouldn't have to worry about them finding her, not that they would have any likelihood while in the community. No one in society even knew it existed.

A fresh wave of anger ran through her. She clutched her hair, ignoring the pain as she pulled against the roots. There were others like her—stolen from their families.

Macy pulled her hair tighter, almost enjoying the pain. She was so furious she wanted to scream. But she knew better. She would have to play nice for just a little bit longer, but she *was* going to find a way out. There was no way she was going to keep living like this.

She slid her fingers out of her hair and got out of bed. She looked outside, seeing no activity. The sun was barely coming up and the frost was especially thick. Macy shivered just looking at it. The room wasn't cold because somehow that wood stove always managed to keep the house warm. Probably because the walls were so thin, as evidenced by her knowing about Chester and Rebekah's nightly routine.

HELD

Sliding the curtain back into place, she paced the room. How was she going to get out? She couldn't do it without a plan. It was too bad she didn't have a bulldozer, then she could just bust through the fence. She paced faster, unable to think of anything realistic.

The last thing she wanted was to spend another week copying the crazy rules. If she had any say, she would find a way to have the community shut down. They had to know that kids had been kidnapped. That would be enough to have Eve and Jonah carted away, wouldn't it? Wasn't that aiding and abetting? With them and Chester gone, surely the community would dissolve.

Not only would she be a lost child returned home, but everyone would cheer for her for saving others just like her. She imagined the big welcome home. Confetti flying in the background. Her parents welcoming her with big smiles and bigger hugs. Alex would look at her adoringly and have nothing to tease her about—he would actually look up to her.

But first she had to get out. After she found a way out of the fence—there had to be a weak spot somewhere—she would run as fast as she could. She had never actually heard any animals outside the fence, so that had to be a myth told to keep people inside. Maybe she could find Chester's gun and take it with her.

She remembered back to when she went into his room at the farmhouse to get her cell phone. That hadn't gone well at all. She'd ended up locked up for nearly long enough to kill her since he hadn't given her any water that time. No. She would have to make her escape without his gun.

There was no way she would take a chance of him locking her up again. She needed a plan of escape that had nothing to do with him or any of his stuff.

The bedroom door opened, startling Macy. She turned around to see Rebekah.

"You're already up. Are you all right?"

Macy took a deep breath. She needed to calm down. "I just had a bad dream."

"Do you want to talk about it?"

"Not really. I suppose it's time to get up. Do we ever get a day off?"

"No. Sorry, Heather. We must work and learn every day. What would

153

happen if the farmers took a day off? Or the prophets? Work is important. It keeps everything moving. Weekends are for the lazy."

Of course.

Rebekah tilted her head. "Are you sure you're okay?"

"I'm fine. I just need to shake off the nightmare."

"If you say so." It was obvious that Rebekah didn't believe her, but she closed the door behind her, giving Macy privacy to change.

Macy yanked off her pajama top and threw it across the room with full force. Being just a shirt, it didn't go far. She pulled off her pants and balled them up and threw them even harder. They bounced off the wall, half landing on the dresser. She slunk down to the ground and dissolved into tears. She pulled her knees up and wrapped her arms around her legs, sobbing as quietly as possible.

She wanted to scream. If she had her way, she would scream at Chester, right in his face. She would pull those big, ugly glasses off, and stomp on them until they were in a million little pieces. Then she would grab him and throw him against the wall, threatening him just like he'd done to her.

Then after beating him up, she would lock him up somewhere to rot until he couldn't go another hour without water. At that point, she would go in there with an ice-cold bottle and hold it just out of reach. Then she would gloat as he begged for it. Once he was in tears, she would drink it in front of him—the entire thing.

After that, he would stop breathing and not be able to hurt anyone ever again.

Anger

MACY SAT AT the table, not looking at Chester or Rebekah. She was too busy planning her escape. Chester yammered on about something, but Macy didn't care.

Anger burned inside of her. She had never hated anyone as much as she hated Chester that moment. She hated him not only for every single thing he had done to her, but also for what he had done to Heather and her mom. Someone so cruel didn't deserve to live, much less be revered by an entire community.

Macy's mom had once told her that people weren't evil, but rather that they only did bad things. Macy knew her mom was wrong about that. Chester was the embodiment of evil. If she believed in a devil, she would think he had come to the earth in the form of a human in Chester.

"Are you listening, Heather?" he asked.

She looked up at him, forgetting to hide her disdain.

"What's that look for? Did I do something to you?"

"She had a bad dream," Rebekah said, too fast.

"Don't cover for her. What's going on, Heather?"

Macy wanted to scream that she wasn't Heather, but she knew that wouldn't get her anywhere except locked up. She took a deep breath and forced her true feelings off her face. "Rebekah's right. I'm in a bad mood because of my dream. I can't shake it."

"Don't take your foul mood out on me. What do you say?"

"What?" Macy asked.

Chester stared at her through his thick, ugly glasses. "When you're rude to someone without cause, there's something you need to say. What is it?"

Macy wanted to punch those glasses right into his skull. Even if her hand ended up bloody and needing stitches, it would be worth it.

"Say sorry," Rebekah whispered.

Not wanting to end up locked up, Macy muttered a barely audible *sorry*.

"What's that? I can't hear you." Chester furrowed his ugly, bushy eyebrows.

Macy pictured his glasses tearing his face apart as she punched him. "I'm sorry I was rude."

"Thank you. Now that wasn't so hard, was it?" He went back to eating his food.

She glared at him before going back to her breakfast. Somehow she made it through the meal without pissing him off or killing him with her bare hands.

On the walk to school, Rebekah was talking about proper behavior, but Macy couldn't pay attention.

She knew Rebekah was only trying to help, but Macy didn't want help. She wanted *out*.

When Macy sat at the desk, Luke gave her a strange look. "Are you okay, Heather?"

The anger built further at being called Heather again. Macy pursed her lips and shook her head.

"What's going on?" he whispered.

She clenched her fists. "I'm going to find a way out of here. Today."

"Whoa. Wait, Heather. You can't just do that." Luke turned and looked directly at her. "Remember what we talked about yesterday? Taking everything slowly and then—"

"You can do that if you want. I'm not waiting. I need to get back to my family, and I'm not waiting ten years. I'm not even waiting a week."

"Think about this first. You can get out with your dad soon. Have you been paying attention what Jonah has been saying about him in the nightly meetings? I know you're not used to the way things usually work, but I've never seen anyone move through the ranks so fast. You won't have to wait long."

A noise caught Macy's attention. Rebekah was standing in front of them, giving them a look of warning. "Is there a problem? You two should be working."

"No problem," Luke said. "I'm just helping Heather to understand the inner workings of the community. She was a little confused on a point."

Rebekah nodded. "Thank you, Luke. I think you're distracting some of the other students, so if you need to continue discussing this, grab Dorcas and you three can have a discussion group outside."

Luke nodded. "Yes, Teacher." He turned to Macy. "Do you need further explanation?"

Macy nodded, too angry to speak.

She went outside with Luke and Dorcas. Luke spoke, but Macy wasn't paying attention. She was looking into the distance to see if the fence was visible, but it was too far away to see anything.

"Do you have a plan?" Dorcas asked.

Macy looked at her. "There has to be a way out. There just has to. It isn't possible for them to have every inch of this place sealed tight."

Luke and Dorcas exchanged a worried look.

"Don't you remember what we told you about the one kid who tried to escape?" Luke asked. "No one knows what happened to him."

Macy clenched her fists. "Maybe because they're embarrassed that he escaped and they couldn't do anything about it."

Dorcas put a hand on Macy's arm. "No. That's not what happened. If you really want out, you've got to have patience."

"Patience? You want patience? You have no idea what I've been through the last few months or however long it's been." She shook her head. "It doesn't matter. I'm done playing by everyone else's rules."

Luke stood taller. "What's your plan?"

"Plan? I have none, except to find a way out of here. The sooner the better."

"I really don't want to see anything happen to you. We need more than that."

"And I don't want to spend another night here. Even if I have to do something extreme, I will."

"Like what?" Dorcas asked, looking worried. "You could get hurt."

"You guys don't have to join me if you don't want to. No need for you to risk yourselves."

"I just need more than what you're giving me," Dorcas said. "Luke and I have had our plan for a long time, and the one thing I like about it is that it's safe."

"And it's too slow. You guys probably have nice families to go home to here, or at least your actual families. I don't have that. All I have is—"

Luke stepped closer. "Shh. Don't talk about it too loud. You're getting worked up. There are lots of kids, even some adults, who have been brought in here that are kidnapped too. You're not alone, but the ones who survive, they take it slowly."

"Where has slow gotten them? They're still here. Some of them have probably either given up or worse, accepted this life. I'm not going to do that."

Luke stared into her eyes, giving her a look that made Macy's heart skip a beat. "You do have people who care about you, even if you don't feel it at home. People who don't want to see you hurt." He took her hand.

Macy swallowed, feeling her anger dissipate. She knew that by *people* he meant himself. Macy didn't want to do anything to put him in danger, either. But what was she supposed to do? There was no way she was going to wait years to escape.

He took another step closer. "I know you're frustrated. You have every right to be. Chester shouldn't have taken you away from your family or brought you here. Life gave you a really unfair hand of cards, but don't do something rash and throw it all away."

Macy stared into his eyes, unable to find her voice.

"Will you take a day to think about it? Maybe when you calm down, you'll be able to think of an actual plan."

"And by then I'll be ready to hide in a corner again, scared and helpless. Who's going to miss me if something does happen? I'll bet you my family already thinks I'm dead."

The look on Luke's face told her that he would be crushed if something happened to her. "Don't go on a suicide mission. Please, Heather."

"My name's—"

Dorcas cleared her throat.

Macy looked up, and Luke let go of her hand, stepping back.

The schoolhouse door opened and Rebekah came outside. She smiled. "How is everything going? Are you getting your questions answered, Heather?"

Macy took a small step back. "Yes. They're really helping me to understand how things work around here."

"Good. Why don't you three come on in? I wouldn't want anyone thinking that you're getting special treatment because of our family situation."

Luke gave Macy a look, almost begging her not to do anything stupid. Her heart fluttered and she looked away. They went inside and she started her copy work, not paying attention to what she was writing. At least her hand had finally adjusted to all the writing.

Her mind was on fire. She was all too aware of Luke sitting next to her, doing his own copying. She wanted to turn and watch him, and that very desire made her angry with herself.

She needed to focus on getting out of the stupid community, not thinking about him. How was that going to help her? And why couldn't she stop thinking about Luke?

Macy's stomach kept doing flip-flops. She didn't feel nervous. What was her problem? She needed to think about Chester and how much she hated him. That was the only way she was going to stay focused on what needed to be done. Thinking about Luke was only distracting her—big time.

The morning dragged on. She didn't care about the work in front of her and she kept wanting to sneak peeks at Luke, and each time she gave in and did, he caught her looking at him.

Macy missed Zoey more than ever. She wanted to talk to her best friend about Luke, the first boy who had ever paid her any real attention. Of course he didn't know that she used to be "Muffin Top Macy." But after everything Chester had put her through, Macy was thinner than ever.

She remembered wanting to be skinny at any cost. How stupid she had been—wishing it at *any* cost. She'd gladly go back to her muffin top if it meant being back home, having never met Chester or his storm shelter where he had starved her until she agreed to take on Heather's identity.

When Rebekah finally announced the morning break, Macy decided she needed to make a run for it as soon as she got outside. Luke was only proving to be a distraction and she needed to get away. No more whining or wishing, it was time for action.

Once she made it outside, she looked around, making sure that no adults were anywhere in sight. The last thing she needed was to run, only to have prophets chase after her. Then she would end up like the one kid who mysteriously disappeared.

Everything was clear, so she burst into a run, heading left, where she was sure the fence was closest. She ducked between a couple of buildings and headed for a group of trees.

Footsteps could be heard from behind. Macy picked up her speed, not looking back. Why hadn't she listened to her parents and joined some kind of sports team? She breathed hard, gasping for air. She hadn't been used to running before Chester took her, and she was in even worse shape after a couple of months of his torture.

Macy looked down, seeing a root sticking up out of the ground, but it was too late. She stumbled over it and went down. It felt like slow motion, but she couldn't do anything to stop from falling. She landed with a hard thud, frost crunching under her.

A hand grasped her shoulder.

Impatience

MACY ROLLED OVER, ready to fight. It was Luke who had her shoulder.

"What are you doing?" he asked.

"I'm finding a way out of here."

He shook his head. "Now?"

She sat up. "Yes, now."

"Can't you at least wait until it's dark?"

"No."

He looked around. "We'd better get back to the schoolhouse."

"I can't go back. I won't."

Luke grabbed her hand and helped her up to stand. "You need to. We'll meet tonight and figure something out."

Her heart raced. She noticed he hadn't let go of her hand. She shook her head. "I don't want to get you in trouble too if it doesn't work out."

"I'm already involved. Let's go."

"But, I can't—"

He walked, taking her along by default. "Your arrival has shown me that I need to step up my plan. I need to get the same fire as I see in your eyes."

"Like I said, I don't want to get you involved."

"And I'm already well past that point." He stopped and turned, looking into her eyes. He took her other hand. "What's your real name?"

"What?"

"I've noticed you flinch when you're called Heather. I want to know your real name."

Did she dare tell him? What if he accidentally called her Macy in front of Rebekah?

"I won't tell anyone. I just want to know who you really are."

She hesitated. "It's Macy Mercer."

"Macy. That's really pretty. It suits you." He squeezed her hands. "We'd better get back before we get into trouble. Then we wouldn't be able to follow our plan tonight, Macy."

Her heart skipped a beat. She liked the way her name rolled off his tongue.

"Okay."

He let go of her hands and they made their way back to the school house.

Rebekah ran up to them before they even crossed the dirt road. "Are you okay, Heather? What happened?"

Macy stared at her, not knowing what to say.

"She got spooked, Teacher. Do you hear the sounds of the farm slaughter?"

Rebekah looked around, appearing to listen. "No."

"Well, it was going on when we came outside," Luke said. "Heather had never heard it before and she thought something was wrong. She didn't even think, only reacted. Right, Heather?"

"Yeah. It scared me. I'm sorry."

Rebekah looked relieved. "Next time something like that happens, please ask someone rather than just taking off." She leaned close to Macy. "We don't need word of this getting back to your dad, you know what I mean?"

"I know. I'm sorry."

"Let's get back into the classroom." She led them back to the schoolhouse, telling the other kids that everything was fine.

Everyone looked at Macy and Luke, but said nothing. Dorcas gave her a knowing and sympathetic look.

When they sat down, Macy's heart still raced. Was it from running, the scare of being chased, or from Luke holding her hands again? Her heart fluttered.

He tapped her foot with his. She looked over at him and he raised an eyebrow and held up his pencil.

"Oh, right." She picked up her pencil and wrote where she'd left off. The rest of the morning dragged on until lunch finally arrived.

On the way back to the house, Rebekah warned Macy not to say anything about running off to Chester. It was obvious by the look on her face that she was still spooked about his tantrum a few weeks earlier.

When Rebekah and Macy sat down to eat lunch, Chester still hadn't arrived. That made her more nervous than if he would have actually been there. "Where is he?"

"He mentioned that Jonah and Abraham might take him out into the world soon to see if they could find anyone needing to join the community. Let me pray."

They bowed their heads and then ate after Rebekah was done with the prayer.

"How long will they be out?" Macy asked.

"Could be until the meeting tonight. It depends on whether or not they find anyone."

Macy tried to mask the excitement. If Chester and Jonah were gone, that might make it even easier to escape.

"Are you feeling better?"

Macy looked at Rebekah, confused.

"You were spooked from hearing the sounds of slaughter, remember?"

"Right. Yeah, I'm fine now." She couldn't tell by the look on Rebekah's face if she believed Luke's story or not. She didn't appear upset if she did doubt. It was also something she didn't want to discuss. "I want to hear more about your band. You told me a little that first morning, but nothing since then."

"I nearly forgot about that." She smiled, looking lost in thought for a moment. "We were really big on the indie scene on the east coast. We were performing in big clubs up and down the coast and had our sights set on Hollywood. But we figured we had a better chance starting out in Seattle. It's big, but not as big, you know?"

Macy nodded, her mouth full of food.

"The lead singer got busted for buying drugs and ratted us out. I was actually running from the cops when I ran into Jonah. They were going to arrest me and I already had a record, so the last thing I wanted was to get caught. He could see the desperation in my eyes. When he told me about the community, I thought it would be the perfect place to hide out for a while."

"But you're still here." Not that she could get out if she wanted to. "Did you ever want to leave?"

Rebekah set her glass down. "At first I was just glad to have somewhere to rest. I was pretty strung out. Eve took care of me for a couple weeks, telling me all about the community the entire time. By the time I had my unveiling and received this house, I was ready to stay. Eve and Jonah both said that I had a lot of potential. Since I had gone to school for teaching, they decided to put that to use."

"So you want to stay here forever? You never think about leaving?"

"This is much better than going to jail. I've been there, and there's nothing desirable. At least here I'm free. I can walk around without a care. Now I can even have a family."

Macy froze. The way that she said family didn't sit right with her. "Are you...expecting?"

Rebekah's face turned red. "It's too soon to tell for sure, but I think so. A woman knows these things. You can't say anything. Your dad wanted to tell you."

Why was Macy surprised? The way they went at it, she was probably carrying a litter. "Well, congratulations." Hopefully it was a little Rebekah, and not a little Chester.

She beamed. "I'm really excited. And I know you'll make a wonderful big sister. Your dad has told me how you've always wanted a sibling."

Macy fought a scowl. She *had* a sibling that she was very happy with, and she was quite eager to get back to him. "Yeah, that'll be great."

Rebekah talked about knitting baby clothes and teaching Macy how to so they could work on it together. Macy nodded, not saying anything. If she had her way, she'd be running through the woods that night looking for the highway.

"We'd better get lunch cleaned up." Rebekah stood up. "Are you all right? You're being quiet."

She forced a weak smile. "Just thinking about how great it's going to be having a baby around."

Rebekah's face lit up. "Oh, good."

They cleaned up and went back to the school. Macy made a beeline for Luke as soon as she saw him. "You haven't chickened out, have you?"

He laughed. The way the skin around his eyes crinkled made Macy melt.

Luke shook his head. "On the contrary." He tilted his head, indicating for her to follow him. Macy followed him to furthest corner of the schoolyard, where the younger kids were milling about.

Luke stood as close to Macy as possible without touching her. "Do you want to know my plan?"

"Tell me."

"We're going to burn down part of the fence and run."

Macy's eyes widened. It was brilliant. "How?"

"With matches of course. I've actually been saving them up. One here and there. I've got quite a collection."

"Why? Stamps aren't good enough for you?"

"I told you, I've been planning on escaping for a long time. I've had several ideas brewing."

"What about waiting twenty years before Jonah would take you outside?"

"That's my long-term plan. I'm not opposed to taking advantage of an opportunity arising, and in fact I've always wanted to be ready for such an event."

"When are we going to do this?"

"The way I see it, we have two options. We can try to sneak out during the meeting, when everyone is distracted or we can wait until everyone is asleep. You stay awake until I tap on your window."

Macy thought about it. "What do you think is better?"

"If Chester is in the spotlight with Jonah, then we shouldn't go then. It's possible they could call you to the front, and once it's discovered that you're missing, all hell is going to break loose. At least at night, everyone will be sleeping."

Butterflies danced in her stomach. They were really going to make a break for it that night.

"What do you think? Can you wait until everyone is sleeping?"

"I sure can."

Mall

"CAN WE GIVE Alex back his electronics?" Alyssa asked. "He's been punished long enough."

Chad looked up from his laptop. He hadn't even heard Alyssa come in.

"This can't go on forever. Especially since he was only trying to protect his sister."

He closed the laptop. "You know that was the agreement to keep him from being suspended."

"Who cares? He doesn't want to go back anyway. I can homeschool him or we can sign him up for that charter school and he can do everything online. I don't want to punish him any more, Chad."

"It's not like we've sent him into exile. Zoey comes over all the time and he's had several of his other friends come by. He's been watching movies with you. He's not without human contact."

Alyssa begged him with her eyes. "Come on. This isn't the time to lay down the law. Look what happened when we were too hard on Macy."

"You're going to bring that up?" Anger ran through him. "This has nothing to do with that, and for your information, if we would have taken away her laptop and phone, guess what? She wouldn't have been *able* to contact that child abductor. She'd still be here."

"Oh, so you don't think she could have borrowed someone's tablet at school and emailed him?"

Chad dug his nails into the desk, not wanting to take out his anger on Alyssa. He was angry enough to break something. He took a deep breath and counted to ten backwards. "Call the school and find out how much longer they want this punishment to last. If it's more than a few days, fine, look into charter schools or homeschooling or whatever you feel like."

"Really?"

"Yeah. While you do that, I need to call Detective Fleshman. You'd think they'd have called about the results from the body. Even if they hadn't found anything yet, they should at least keep us in the loop."

"No news is good news, right?" Alyssa asked. She turned around and left, closing the door behind her.

Chad picked up his phone and called Fleshman, who answered right away. "Chad, I wish I had answers for you. As I told you, your family's dental records were in the part of the office that was destroyed by the fire and they didn't keep those online."

"I know that!" Chad stood up, sending his wheeled chair into the wall. "Surely, you have something to tell me. I'm not waiting for takeout—this is my daughter's life."

"We're doing everything we can. It's out of our hands now that the body has been sent to Seattle. We're anxious to know the results too, but this isn't TV. DNA results don't come back in five minutes. There's a lot to consider. They're running the girl's fingerprints through the system, but again, everything takes time—weeks, usually."

"What else are you doing? Besides waiting on Seattle?"

"We're going through all the clues. Have you seen the room we have dedicated to Macy's case? Even with my entire team focused on it, nothing is moving as fast as any of us would like. I have a son, Chad. I can imagine what you're going through. If it was my boy missing, I'd be pulling my hair out. I'm working as diligently as if it was him."

Chad let out long, slow breath. "I do appreciate everything you guys are doing."

"And I answer your calls day or night, whether I'm at work or home."

"Am I bothering you at home?"

"You're not bothering me, Chad."

So he *was* calling him at home. "I don't want to keep you. Can you call me when you're on the clock?"

"I'd be glad to."

"Thanks." He hung up and looked around his office. It felt suffocating. In fact, the entire house did. He went upstairs and found Alyssa on the phone. "What's going on?" he asked.

"The school has me on hold."

"I'm going to the store. Need anything?"

She shook her head. "Did you hear anything?"

"Still waiting on Seattle, because tests take time and our dentist is an idiot."

"Yes, I'm still here," Alyssa said into the phone.

Chad waved and headed for the door. He knew he probably looked like a wreck, but he didn't even care enough to grab a baseball cap. Everyone knew who he was thanks to the news, so no one would give it a second thought if he looked tired and stressed.

He got into his car and drove to the grocery store. Once parked, he sat in the car for a few minutes. They didn't need anything. What was he doing there? Was he going to wander around, squeezing melons? Comparing prices? That was ridiculous. The mall wasn't so far away. He could at least wander and window shop.

Not only that, but that's where Macy's clothes and phone had been found. Maybe he could find a new clue.

Chad turned the ignition and drove to the mall. He parked as far away as possible and meandered through the parking lot, starting with the edge, looking for anything that could be a clue. There was nothing other than random litter, probably dropped from people leaving the movie theater.

He made his way to the entrance, looking for a valuable piece of evidence. He couldn't allow himself to miss anything. If there was anything he could do to help Macy, he had to do it.

Eyes still to the ground, he went inside. He hadn't seen anything other than trash, and given that they had a janitorial staff, anything useful would have been cleaned up and removed. He took his attention from the ground and looked around at the stores. Nothing interested him—how could it?

As he meandered, Chad noticed people whispering. Now he regretted not grabbing a baseball cap. He could've lowered it over his face to get attention away from him.

He would just have to ignore them, as uncomfortable as it was. Then a thought hit him: this must have been what Macy felt like at school. Only worse, being young and not understanding the nature of people who apparently didn't grow up just because they got older. Chad noticed ladies in their fifties whispering and pointing at him.

Way to outgrow high school, ladies, he thought sarcastically.

Maybe the mall hadn't been a good idea. Eyes burned his back, so he picked up his pace. His stomach was rumbling and he couldn't even remember the last time he ate. Chad headed for the courtyard. He ordered some burritos and sat down at a table in the corner.

People appeared to be more interested in their food than him at least. Just as he bit down, someone stopped next to the table. He groaned and looked up.

Lydia stood there, looking at him with a pitiful expression. "Mind if I sit?"

Chad swallowed his food. "I thought I made myself clear. We can't do this anymore."

"Can't we just have a seat at the same table? We're neighbors. No one is going to question anything. I've been so worried about you. The news—"

"Fine. Sit. I'm not going to be here long anyway."

She sat and ate from her own tray of food.

Chad noticed she had gotten a haircut, but he knew better than to say anything.

"You don't look so good, Chad. How are you holding up? The news—"

"I really don't want to talk about the news. It's a four letter word in our house these days." He tried to avoid her dark, beautiful eyes. He knew he was predisposed to pouring out his soul to her.

That had been what had gotten him into trouble in the first place. Alyssa was shutting him out, and Lydia was so eager to hear anything he had to say. Dean was almost never home and even when he was, he didn't pay attention to Lydia. It was a perfect setup.

"Do you need anything?" she asked.

"My daughter."

"You don't think that girl they found—?"

"No!" He bit into his burrito. Coming to the mall definitely had been a bad decision.

"I'm sorry. I've really missed you. We always had the best—"

"Lydia," Chad hissed. He looked around to make sure no one was paying any attention to them.

"I was going to say we have the best talks." She rolled her eyes. "I could always tell you anything, and you never judged me. It went both ways."

"I'm talking to Alyssa now. You should try opening up to Dean. Rekindle whatever it was that attracted you two in the first place."

She shook her head. "I've tried. I'm certain that he's seeing someone else."

"Then dump his sorry butt. He doesn't know what he's missing. You deserve better, but I can't be the one to give you what you do deserve. I'd be lying if I said otherwise. You're smart, you're fun, and you're talented. There are a lot of guys out there who would be more than happy to give you what Dean won't."

Lydia tugged on a strand of thick, dark hair. "I can't move on."

"Dean would have to give you spousal support since you've been a housewife all this time. You wouldn't be out of money."

"That's not what I mean. Sure, the money is why I stay, but I meant I can't move onto another man when I'm still in love." Lydia stared into his eyes.

Chad returned the stare, but with wide eyes. She was *in love* with him? They'd had a good thing before he cut her off—and it hadn't been easy. But he never would have guessed she was in love.

She continued to stare at him with eagerness in her eyes.

If he said one word, Lydia would bring him back to her large, empty house in a heartbeat. Chad cleared his throat. "I should probably get back home. I just came here to uh…um, look for clues."

"Are you Scooby Doo now?"

"Tell Dean I said hi."

Lydia frowned. "I guess you're not the mood to joke around."

Chad narrowed his eyes. "No, actually I'm not." He looked around and lowered his voice. "I'm a family man. I made a *mistake*."

She looked like she had been slapped.

"And I'm sorry I hurt you. Really I am. Like I said, you deserve a lot better—than both Dean and me. Alyssa deserves better too and given our history and the fact that we have a family together, I'm doing whatever I can to be that for her now."

"That's exactly why I'm having such a hard time moving on. I wish Dean was the kind of man that you are."

"Maybe if you show him the kind of attention you gave me, he'll come around." He finished off the burrito, eager to get through the next one. Lydia didn't look like she was planning to leave the table anytime soon.

As he unwrapped the last burrito, he saw Sandra McMillan, another neighbor. She was headed their way.

Chad's heart sank. Would she tell Alyssa that she'd seen Chad eating with Lydia?

Sandra waved and sat down. Her big, blonde hair nearly took up the entire table. "All we need is a few more neighbors and we would have an impromptu HOA meeting." She laughed loudly.

Lydia gave a fake smile—Chad could see right through it. "Good one," Lydia said. "How are you, Sandra?"

"Pretty good. Just trying to figure out how to get the new family in 1612 to remove those hideous flamingos. Can you believe them?"

"They're awful," Lydia said, though it was obvious that Lydia couldn't have cared less.

Sandra turned to Chad, her makeup-heavy eyes wide. "And how are you doing, sweetie?" She continued on, not giving him a chance to answer. "I've been talking with some of the other neighbors about forming another search party, but I wanted to find out what you guys want. What with everything the news has been saying lately." She shook her head. "The whole thing is awful, just awful."

Chad shoved as much burrito into as mouth as he could. At least Sandra was oblivious to the tension between Lydia and Chad.

Not even stopping to take a breath, Sandra turned back to Lydia. "And how is Dean? I haven't seen him at a meeting in so long. Does he still travel for work? Where is he now, dear?"

"He's in Siberia at the moment. Then he'll be off to India, and then Germany before he comes home to have some dinner and leave again."

Sandra patted Lydia's hand. "You poor, poor thing. You must get so lonely." She shook her head. "It's just too bad you two can't have any kids. They would be the perfect distraction for you."

Lydia and Chad exchanged a look. How could Sandra be so dense? That was a topic that ripped Lydia's heart out, and even if it wasn't, that was such an insensitive thing to say.

Chad swallowed the last of his food and stood up. "It was nice running into you ladies, but I need to get back home to my family."

Telling

ZOEY ROLLED OVER in bed. Her entire body ached and she just wanted to go back to sleep. Though she'd slept most of the day, she didn't feel like she had. Her mind raced, chasing sleep away.

Had they found anything out about that body? Her mom said that the chances weren't likely that it was Macy and not to worry about it. How would she know? No one knew anything.

Valerie was obviously worried about Zoey. She hadn't even made her go back to school since the body was found. She had also been on the phone with Zoey's dad every day. The night before, she'd wanted Zoey to talk with him, but Zoey refused. What was she supposed to say?

Her bedroom door opened and her mom came in. "Oh, good. You're awake. I just got off the phone with your dad, and he said as soon as he officially retires, he's coming here. He's been talking with the coach, explaining that he has a family crisis and that with his injury, he can't play anyway."

Zoey rolled her eyes. "So?"

"I want you to be prepared."

"He's the one who needs to be prepared," she muttered.

Valerie raised an eyebrow. "What does that mean?"

Zoey sat up. "That I'm going to give him a piece of my mind. Forget a piece—he's getting the whole thing. He's never been here for me, and I don't need him now."

"That's not entirely fair. It was an agreement that we had for him to stay there."

"So then you're equally at fault. But at least you've been here."

"He hasn't been completely absent. He's sent money all these years when he didn't have to."

"That's not being a father. He's a sperm donor and nothing more."

"Zoey! You'd better not talk to him like this when he gets here."

"Then you should tell him to stay in Japan, because I'm not holding back."

"He wants to be a part of your life."

"So all it took was me getting knocked up? Why didn't you tell me that sooner? I could have done that two and a half years ago."

Her mom sighed. "Obviously, he can't change the past, but he wants to make good on everything now."

"Sure. His career is over. If it was going strong, he wouldn't care about me, would he?"

"He's always cared. If he didn't—"

"Then he wouldn't have sent the money. Got it. It's too little, too late."

"Just give him a chance."

"Why?" Angry tears filled her eyes. "Why should I? Just because he supplied some DNA and sent some money? Now he feels guilty because I'm going to make him a grandparent. Except that he's not going to be a grandparent. You know why? Because he would have to be a dad first, and he's not! Unless he's gone and had kids with some other chick, guess what. He's not a dad. He's certainly not one to me."

Her mom sat on the bed. "I know you're having a hard time, and you have all those hormones making it worse, but please give him a chance. If you want to be mad at someone, be mad at me."

"If I *want* to be mad? I just want to be happy. Actually, no. You really want to know what I want?"

"What?"

"A cigarette."

Her mom's eyes widened, and her face turned pale. "What?" she whispered.

"That's right! I've been smoking, and that's the one thing I actually want. You wouldn't believe the havoc not having any has wrecked upon my body."

Her mom stared, not saying a word.

Zoey's eyebrows came together. *Good. Hit her where it really hurt.*
"You've really been smoking?"

"Yeah. Want to make something of it?" Zoey squeezed her covers.

"Even after your uncle died of cancer?"

"Yes. And I know how you feel about smoking, but I did it anyway. Turns out I'm pretty good at keeping secrets too. Wonder where I got it from?" Zoey narrowed her eyes.

Valerie got up without a word and left the room.

Zoey felt a little bad, but her mom had it had it coming.

She picked up her phone to check for texts. Alex hadn't sent her anything. She sent him a text asking if he was awake. Then she remembered that his parents had taken all of his stuff away after he'd posted Macy's diary entries.

When would he get those back? It was like living in the days before electricity. How did anyone survive before laptops and cell phones? Kids must have sneaked out way more back in those days. It was totally barbaric.

Her phone buzzed, startling her. She had a text from Alex: *He's still grounded, but hopefully will have his stuff back today. You're more than welcome to come over.*

Zoey smiled. *Thanks, Alyssa.* At least someone had a mom who got it.

She put her phone away. Going to the Mercer's house sounded like a good idea. It would be a lot better than hanging out with her mom. Especially after Zoey told her about the cigarettes.

She got into the shower and then went downstairs to find something to eat that wouldn't make her stomach turn. Wasn't pregnancy supposed to make people eat and eat? She had already lost ten pounds because everything sounded gross. Even her favorite foods had been making her gag at the thought of eating them.

As she looked through the pantry and the fridge, nothing looked good. She would probably lose more weight, because she wasn't going to eat anything that made her gag.

Zoey went to the door and put on a pair of shoes.

"Where do you think you're going?"

She looked up to see her mom standing at the end of the hall, hands on her hips.

"Over to the Mercers."

"No, you're not."

"Yes, I am." Zoey stared at her, daring Valerie to try to stop her.

"Not after the way you treated me up there."

"What? All I did was tell you the truth."

"How long?"

"How long what?"

"Don't give me that. How long have you been smoking?"

"I don't know. A while."

"You don't know? How could you not know?"

"Well, it's not like I wrote down the date of my first one. I'm not going to throw a party on the anniversary."

"Shut up, Zoey. Clearly I'm not looking for an exact date. *About* how long have you been smoking?"

"I really don't know. Okay? When Macy and I got scheduled for opposite lunch periods, I found some new kids to hang out with. They always went out to smoke. At first, I just went with them. Then one day I tried one and hated it. I didn't go near them for a while, but then at some point I tried again."

"What made the difference?"

Alex. Not that she was going to rat him out.

"Whatever, Zoey. Don't answer me. Where were you able to smoke at school? They have strict policies against drugs."

Zoey snorted. "The policies may be strict, but they don't enforce them. There's a big space in the blackberry bushes between the high school and junior high. That's where the smokers go. That and under the bleachers when it rains. Can I go now?"

"Why? Why would you start smoking? Especially after seeing everything your uncle went through?"

"Because sometimes I do things just because I want to, or because I want to make my friends happy." She stared at her mom, daring her to keep going with the conversation.

"Some things are no-brainers, and this is one of them. You saw what he went through."

"Doesn't mean I'll go through it myself."

Valerie took a deep breath, looking away. It looked like she was counting silently. "Do you promise not to go back to smoking?"

Zoey grabbed her aching head. "I'm not going to make a promise I can't keep."

"Zoey!"

"Can I go now?"

"Maybe you should tell Alex about your smoking. He could probably talk some sense into you. At least you would listen to him."

"Okay, I'll do that. Can I go?"

Valerie waved her toward the door, looking away again.

Zoey got out as fast as she could, before she could give her mom a chance to start talking again. She breathed in the crisp, cold air. As she walked down the sidewalk, she looked up at the sky and saw a cloud that looked like a pouncing cat. Zoey couldn't help remembering all the stories she and Macy had made up about cloud animals over the years.

Was Macy okay? Was it possible that she was happy? Maybe she was; she just couldn't get a hold of anyone since she didn't have her phone.

Blinking back tears, Zoey walked up to the Mercer's door. Zoey almost knocked, but suddenly felt overwhelmed with grief. She wanted Macy more than ever. They had always talked over everything in each other's lives. So much had happened in such a short time, and Zoey hadn't been able to tell her best friend any of it.

She sat on the steps and cried into her hands. She didn't need her dad—she'd gotten along just fine without him all this time. What she needed was Macy. It was great being able to talk with Alex, and Zoey couldn't have asked for a better boyfriend, but he still wasn't Macy.

He was also just as close to everything as Zoey was. His sister was missing and he was the baby's father. For all the new friends she had made over the last year or so, there wasn't one that she wanted to talk to about any of this.

Sniffling, she wiped her eyes and nose. She didn't want anyone to see her like this. She looked across the street, having forgotten to check for the media van. It wasn't there, but she thought she saw the back of a police car.

Her stomach twisted, making her feel nauseated. Zoey leaned against the nearest post, trying to imagine life a year from now if Macy was still gone. She'd have had a baby with Alex.

What if Macy was back by then? If so, would she be mad at Zoey for putting her baby brother in this situation?

New tears filled her eyes and she continued to look around the yard through her blurry vision. Images flooded her mind of climbing the tree with Macy. How many times had they pretended that Alex was the bad guy? They had thrown water balloons, balls, and so much more at him from those branches over the years, laughing and squealing the entire time.

Sure, those days were over because they were all teenagers—and other reasons she didn't want to think about.

More tears spilled onto her face and she sobbed into her hands again. "Macy, please come back. I need you."

Worried

ALEX LOOKED UP, feeling guilty when the door to Macy's room opened. He knew that it wasn't Macy coming in as he read through her diary. It was his mom, and she looked more troubled than usual.

"I'm just looking for clues," Alex said, holding up the diary. "There might be something in one of these that—"

"You're fine, baby. I appreciate you going through those. I can't bring myself to read them right now. That's not why I'm in here. Have you heard from Zoey?"

Alex sat up, dropping the journal. "Is something wrong?"

"I hope not. Valerie just called looking for her. She left upset hours ago, and she was headed here."

He jumped off the bed. "She hasn't called or texted. I've had my phone since you gave it back."

"That's what I figured. I'll call Valerie back and let her know we haven't seen her."

Alex ran for the door. "I'm going to look for her."

"She could be anywhere. Don't get yourself lost too."

"I'm not. I can think of several places she might be if she's mad at her mom. I don't know why she wouldn't have come here first, though."

"Maybe she just wanted some alone time."

"I hope." Fear tore through Alex. What if something had happened to her too? He couldn't lose both his sister and his girlfriend.

Alex grabbed a coat from his room and then stopped by the front door to get his shoes on. As he ran out the door, he nearly tripped over Zoey, who was sitting on the top step.

He stared at her with a mix of disbelief and relief. "What are you doing out here? It's way too cold." He sat down, wrapping his arms around her. Her skin was as cold as the air. "Let's go inside."

She shook her head.

"How long have you been here? Your mom said you left hours ago."

Zoey shrugged her shoulders.

Alex took his coat off and put it over her. "What's wrong?"

"What *isn't* wrong? That's what I want to know."

He shivered. "Now that you have my jacket, can we go inside?"

She gave him an exasperated look. "Fine."

Alex helped her up and into the house. "Mom! I found Zoey."

Alyssa ran down the stairs. "Oh, good. I'm so glad you're okay." She gave Zoey a hug. "I'd better call your mom."

Zoey made a face. "Please don't. I don't want her coming over here."

"But she's worried. I know what that feels like."

"Please, Alyssa. I really don't want to see her now. I really, really don't."

"Then I'll just call her and say that Alex went out and found you. Does that work?"

"Thank you."

After getting their shoes off, Alex helped her into the kitchen. "Let me make you some coffee, okay? You need to warm up."

"I'm not drinking coffee."

"Hot cocoa, then. Are you hungry? I can warm you up leftovers. We always have something." He filled a coffee cup with milk and stuck it in the microwave.

"No. Food just makes me sick."

"You should eat something. You can't starve."

"It's better than puking." She stared at a wall.

Alex thought he should change the subject. "I've been reading Macy's diaries. She might hate me for it when she comes back, but I'm hoping there might be something in there to help us find her."

"Are you going to post those entries online too?" Her voice sounded flat.

"Not after losing my electronics."

"Have you found anything?"

"Not yet, but I might not be looking close enough. I haven't even found her most recent one."

The microwave beeped and Alex took out the hot mug. He scooped in half a dozen spoonfuls of cocoa mix before stirring and then setting it in front of Zoey. He sat next to her, in Macy's chair. "There could still be clues in them. Given the circumstances, I think it's okay to read them. It's not like I'm going to use anything against her, you know."

She shrugged and then picked up the mug, taking a sip. "That's really rich."

"But it's good. You know it is." He gave her a playful grin, hoping to get a smile out of her. He could always make her smile.

Zoey stared at him for a moment before she finally cracked a small smile. She drank the rest of the hot chocolate in silence.

"Want to go up to my room? I can tell you what I read."

"Sure." She went to the sink and rinsed the cup out. They walked up to his room in silence, holding hands.

Sounds of a newscast could be heard coming from the bonus room.

Alex sighed. "Why does Mom do that to herself?"

Zoey gave him a confused look.

"She watches the news and then just gets upset about when they say anything about Macy. Though they haven't had much to say lately, barely giving her a mention these days. It seems like that upsets Mom just as much as when the news was nearly all about her."

"It could be her way of looking for clues."

"Maybe." He opened his door. "Sorry for the mess."

"Why? It's always messy."

Alex felt his cheeks heat up. "I'm too busy with other stuff to worry about cleaning. Do you think I should pick up?"

She sat on his bed, leaning against the headboard. "Do what you want."

He went around and sat next to her. "You're still so cold." He pulled his blankets over her and snuggled against her. "You know you can tell me anything, right?"

Zoey grunted, making it obvious that she didn't want to talk.

"Well, I've been reading Macy's diaries since I got up. Not that it's been all that long." He looked at his window, seeing that it was already starting to get dark. "I was tempted to post more pictures of entries about those jerks bullying her, but if I post anything else, my parents will probably sell my phone."

"Nothing about Jared or plans to move to Hollywood?"

"Hollywood? Did she ever say—?"

"No. Just throwing it out there."

"You don't have any ideas where she would go?" he asked.

"Definitely not Clearview."

"What if that's where Jared lives? Maybe she fell for a farm boy."

"Did you see that selfie on his profile? That was no farmer."

Alex shrugged. "Well, it's possible that kids in Hickville aren't wearing overalls with pieces of hay in their mouths."

Zoey leaned her head against his shoulder. "Do you really think she's still alive?"

"I have to."

"Me too. But I keep going back and forth. Sometimes I think she's off somewhere, living a good life. Then I get pissed. How dare she leave without saying goodbye? But then, what if, like, she saw something bad and the witness protection took her and said she had to make a clean break? Or what if something bad did happen to her? Then I'm a huge jerk for being pissed."

Alex took her hand and slid his fingers between hers. "I'm sure she'd understand. She'd be going through all the same stuff if one of us was missing instead of her."

"I hate not knowing. It's the worst."

He kissed the top of her head. "I know."

"What if we never know? How are we supposed to move on with our lives?"

"I have no idea. I hope we don't have to figure that out. I just keep thinking about the kids that were kidnapped and were found after a long time. There was that one girl who was gone almost a year. My parents keep talking about her. Then there was another one who was gone a really long time. More than ten years, I think. Even if Jared did kidnap her, she could turn up one day."

"But what are we supposed to do in the meantime?"

"The people who bring our food keep talking about praying. I'm starting to think maybe that's what we should do."

Zoey looked at him, raising an eyebrow. "You do?"

"It couldn't hurt, could it? What if there's a God and he's just waiting for us to ask him for help?"

Zoey looked uncomfortable. "What does your shrink say?"

"To think positive thoughts."

"Have you?"

He shrugged and looked away. "It's hard. She's gone, and it doesn't make any sense. How could any good have come from whatever happened to her? If she was okay, she'd have let us know somehow. Sure, she could be a brat at times, but she wouldn't do this to us. Not on purpose."

"So you think praying is the answer then?"

"I don't know. It wouldn't hurt to try, I guess."

"Maybe. But if there was a God, why would he have let this happen in the first place?"

Alex thought about everything he'd heard from the people bringing meals to their house. "They said he doesn't interfere with free will, even if it brings heartache. But if we ask for help, he'll provide."

"That doesn't make any sense."

"It kind of does."

"Good luck with that. Let me know if you try." Zoey twisted her hair around and pulled an elastic band from her wrist, tying up her hair into a masterpiece.

Alex stared in amazement at her hair. How had she done that without a mirror? Even the way a few random strands hung loosely, it looked like a work of art, framing her ears and face.

She gave him a curious look. "What?"

"You're beautiful."

"Oh, stop."

"No, really. You are." He reached over and pulled a strand behind her ear. He let the back of his hand slide down her cheek, neck, and down to her stomach. Alex felt a slight bump on her stomach. His eyes lit up. "Is that…the baby?"

She nodded.

He slid her shirt up, exposing the bump. Holding his breath, he ran his hand over it. Finally, he breathed. "That's amazing."

"I guess."

"You don't think so?" He looked into her beautiful eyes, not moving his hands from her belly.

"It's hard when I feel so gross. I just feel bloated."

"Do you feel it moving around?"

"Nope. Doctor says it's too early."

Alex put his ear to the bump.

"I don't think you'll hear anything." Zoey laughed.

He kissed it and then sat up. "You never know."

"It's weird to think we'll be parents. Even if we don't keep it, we'll still be the parents."

"Do you want to?" Alex rubbed the bump again.

"Keep it?" Zoey asked. "I'm not sure. I keep thinking about what happened to your aunt and uncle. I don't want to do that."

Alex's aunt and uncle hadn't been able to have a baby, but they were all set to adopt a baby. Then after the baby was born, the mom had changed her mind. His aunt and uncle went home to an empty nursery. It had destroyed them and they eventually divorced.

"So, you want to wait until you give birth to decide?" Alex asked.

"Possibly. I know we're young and everything, but people raise babies in high school. You know there's a daycare in the back of the school, don't you?"

"I didn't."

"What do you want to do?"

"Me?" Alex asked. "It's up to you."

"Not entirely. Even if I wanted to give it up, you could still decide you want to raise the baby."

He let out a slow breath. All of a sudden, thirteen felt so young. "We have lots of time to figure this out. Maybe by then, Macy will even be able to give us her opinion."

Zoey didn't look convinced. "Maybe."

Fire

MACY PACED HER room, sweating. She had on several layers of white clothes, not knowing how long they would be outside. It was sometime in January, but she didn't know when since the community didn't celebrate holidays or even keep the same calendar.

It had to be close to the end of January, because at the meeting that night Jonah had gone on and on about anointing Chester as a prophet. Chester was supposed to become a prophet before spring. All that was left was that he convert someone from the world, and they had apparently met someone with potential earlier that day when they were out in the world.

Chester would be pissed when Macy escaped. That would probably ruin his chances at becoming a prophet. Not only would she have run away, but part of their precious fence would be gone, allowing anyone to leave if they wanted.

At the meeting, Luke kept making eye contact with her. He was as ready as she was to get out of there. Possibly more, since he had been planning this since long before Macy ever became part of the community.

She put her ear to the door, making sure that no one was up. Rebekah and Chester had finished their nightly ritual nearly an hour before.

Macy looked out the window. Where was Luke? She was going to have to remove some of her layers soon.

What if something had gone wrong? Her heart dropped at the thought. What if he had been caught and was locked away somewhere? What if he would never be seen again? Then it would be all her fault. If he got hurt, it was on her. She would have to live with that for the rest of her life.

Even though he did want to escape, this hadn't been his plan. He was willing to wait decades if that was what it took. But it was easier for him. He was at least with his mom. Macy was with a psychopath who she hated more every moment of every day.

Something hit her window, startling her. She looked out the curtain, but didn't see anything. It was too dark. But it had to be Luke. Who else would it be? Unless he had been caught and this was a trick. Macy narrowed her eyes, still not seeing anything. A porch light would have been helpful, but she would have to take her chances.

If Luke had been caught, he wouldn't have ratted her out. She took a deep breath and then walked to her door. Her heart pounded in her ears. That was going to make it hard to hear if Chester was up. She pulled the door open and it didn't make a sound.

Macy held her breath and tip-toed down the hall. She peeked into the living room, half-expecting to see Chester sitting on the couch. It was empty. In fact, she could hear him snoring down the hall.

She walked through the room and stopped in front of the door. "Please open quietly." She turned the knob, almost expecting sirens to wail, even though she knew there was no electricity for miles.

Macy went outside and closed the door as slow as possible, in disbelief that she was actually outside on her own. She couldn't see anything, but followed the path by memory. When she got to the edge of the property, someone grabbed her arm.

"Luke?"

"Yes. Let's hurry. I haven't seen anyone, but that doesn't mean we won't. I know a path we can take that doesn't get used often." He moved his hand down her arm and caressed her palm. Then he slid his fingers through hers. "Come on."

Macy followed him as best she could, trying to keep up in the dark.

After a few minutes, he said, "Here's the path."

"How can you see anything?"

"I stood outside for a while until my eyes adjusted. It helps that I know this place well. We're going to go a bit further until we get to a spot that's far enough from any homes that no one will hear the fire until we have a chance to get away."

"Are we just going to run to the highway?"

"Better than that. I've got my mom's car keys. I hope it still runs after all these years. If it doesn't, then yeah, we'll run."

"Do you know how to drive?"

"No. Do you?"

"I'm only fifteen."

"Well, I've driven a tractor for Farmer Jeremiah. It can't be all that different."

"Let's hope. What about Dorcas? She didn't want to take part in it?"

"She's actually acting as our lookout while we start the fire."

"Is she going to go with us?"

"If she can. If not, she's going to cover for us and continue the plan to go out with the prophets one day. She said that either way, she's happy for us."

"Okay." Macy followed him in silence as they made their way through the path. She found that the moon and the stars were actually helpful in helping her eyes adjust. "How much further?"

"We're almost there."

Macy swallowed. Her throat was dry and her heart was steadily increasing speed. Was she really going to be free from Chester? It was almost too much to think about.

"There's the fence."

She narrowed her eyes, looking for it. She saw something in the distance, but wasn't sure if it was the fence or not. It had to have been, it was the only thing she could see that wasn't part of the path. They made their way through the path and ended up face to face with the tall structure, the wire at the top gleaming in the moonlight.

Luke dug through his pockets and pulled out box of matches. "It's the moment of truth. Are you ready?"

"More than you know."

"I'm sure you are, Macy." He gave her a sad smile. "Let's get you to your family."

"What about you? What are you going to do when get to civilization?"

"Don't worry about me. I'm almost eighteen and I have a lot of skills. I can get a job and possibly a formal education."

A branch snapped in the distance. Macy froze, staring at Luke. "What was that?"

"Probably just Dorcas. She's looking out for us, remember?"

"I haven't even seen her. Are you sure?"

"Yes. She knows the drill. If anyone approaches, she's going to blow a whistle. Then you and me, we run."

Macy took a deep breath. "Okay. Let's go. I just want to get out of here."

He nodded and then took a step closer to the fence. Looking around, he pulled a match from the box.

Another branch snapped. Macy wasn't so sure that it was Dorcas, but she was afraid to speak her doubts.

Luke held the match to the bottom of the fence.

Macy had imagined the match causing an instant, huge fire, but it wasn't catching at all. Another branch snapped and she jumped toward Luke, nearly crashing into him. He didn't seem to notice.

"Can you find some twigs?" he asked. "We'll need to light some of those first to get the fire going."

"Sure." She found some not too far away and handed them over. "Let me light some of those."

He passed her a match and then the box. She struck the match and gave him back the box. She held a twig up to the match and watched as it lit up. Luke stuck his lit up twig at the bottom of the fence and Macy followed suit. He gave her another match and then added more twigs to the bottom of the fence.

She watched, hoping that one of them would ignite the fence. The more time that passed, the more nervous she became. Beads of sweat broke out on her forehead despite being able to see her labored breath. If they got caught before they could escape, they were going to end up in all kinds of trouble—if not dead.

Luke blew on the twigs, so she bent down and did the same. One of his twigs' fire caught and a tiny part of the fence lit up. It was practically nothing, but she gave him a high five.

He bent down and blew on another twig. "Let's get the rest of these lit up. This is taking too long."

Macy lowered herself to the frosty ground and blew on the twigs nearest her. One of them caught on the fence, the flame moving ever so slowly up the tall beam. She moved to the next one and before long, a length about five feet of the fence was engulfed in flames.

Another branch snapped. This time, right behind them.

Heart pounding, Macy turned around. Chester stood, staring at them. The small flame reflected in his glasses.

A choked sound escaped from Macy's throat. Luke turned around, fear covering his face.

"What are you doing?" Chester demanded.

Luke grabbed Macy's arm and ran, pulling her along with him. She ran, all too aware of Chester's footsteps behind them. How had he found them?

She looked back and saw that he wasn't far behind. Macy picked up her pace, her legs burning. She didn't care, she had to keep going. But how were they going to get away now? Were they going to have to kill him? Was that even possible?

Luke took an unexpected turn in between a couple of buildings. He pulled her along as they zigged and zagged through more buildings. They needed to lose Chester or neither of them would see the next day. Macy had no idea where they were or how to get away.

They continued darting in between different buildings and then ended up down another path and eventually headed into a field of corn. There were small, narrow paths and their shoulders brushed the corn stalks as they ran. Macy thought she heard Chester behind them, but she couldn't be sure. It was hard to hear over the stalks scraping against her clothes.

Her throat was even drier than it had been before. Her legs were on fire, burning all the way up and down and even making its way up to her chest. That too felt like as though engulfed in flames. She'd had no chance to exercise over the last couple months and it showed. She pushed through, forcing herself to keep up with Luke.

"I can hear you two!" Chester shouted. He sounded pretty close.

Luke stopped and Macy ran into him. He put his hand up to his lips and then he sat on the ground, pulling her down too. They sat and Macy gasped for air, trying to breathe without making a sound.

"If he can hear us," Luke whispered, tickling her ear, "we're better off staying put. He'll have a harder time finding us, plus you need to rest."

She nodded, afraid to speak. If Chester found them, he might kill them—if he still had his gun or knife. Had he been able to get them past the prophets when they moved in? If so, they were definitely dead. If he went for help, that would give them a small window of time to get away.

Macy didn't know where they were in relation to the fence. Obviously, being in the middle of a corn field, they had to be pretty far from it. She looked at Luke, who appeared to be deep in thought.

Chester yelled something, but Macy couldn't understand what he said. He must have moved further away from them.

"What are we going to do?" she whispered.

Luke looked at her. "Let's wait a minute. It sounds like he's moving away from us. We're going to have to go the other way, which will put us at a different part of the fence than we were, and we're going to have to start over with the fire.

"Do you think we're still going to be able to get away?"

"Yes. I have my doubts about getting to the parking lot, though. Will you be able to make it to the highway if we have to run?"

"I'll do whatever I have to do. I didn't even know that you were planning on taking a car."

Leaves rustled nearby. Macy froze.

Running

DORCAS APPEARED IN front of them. "You two are difficult to find." She sounded out of breath. "Sorry about Chester. He snuck around a way I didn't see."

"Where is he now?" Luke asked.

"He's gone that way." Dorcas pointed to the left.

"So we're definitely going to have to run for a different part of the fence," Luke said.

"What's going to happen if he catches us?" Dorcas' eyes were wide.

Luke grabbed Macy's hand and squeezed. "He's not."

"But what if he does, Luke?" Dorcas asked. "You guys have to plan for that."

"I'll fight him off and let you and Macy run."

"Macy?" Dorcas looked confused for a moment. "Oh, her real name. All you have is matches, right?"

"Don't worry. My street smarts have stuck with me, Dorcas. You need to get Macy away from him if I end up fighting him. He kidnapped her. Who knows what else he's capable of? She has to get away even if I don't."

Macy gasped. "No."

Luke pulled her closer, wrapping his arm around her. Despite the fear shooting through her, his embrace was comforting. He looked into her eyes. "I knew the risks when we made the plans."

The blood drained from Macy's face. "But I—"

He shook his head. "Don't worry about it. When I saw how desperate you were to get away this morning, I knew I needed to help you."

"I'm sorry. I'm so sorry. I didn't want to put you in danger."

Dorcas frowned. "It's not time for remorse. We're past that. You two are in deep; Chester hasn't seen me yet, but I promised to do what I can to protect you guys, and I will."

"Can you hear him?" asked Luke.

They all sat in silence. Macy couldn't hear anything above their breathing.

Dorcas looked at Luke. "Either he's too far away to hear or he's sitting still like we are, waiting for us to make a move."

Luke nodded. "Let's wait a little longer. If he's waiting for us to make a move, I want to disappoint him."

Macy leaned closer to Luke, feeling both comforted and energized in his arms. She noticed her shoulder moving along with his breathing; she was breathing in tune with him.

"What are we going to do?" Macy asked. "I feel like we're sitting ducks."

"Wait just a bit longer," Luke said. "We need to be patient. I want to be sure that he's not waiting close by for us." He pulled out the box of matches and took some out. Then he handed Macy the box.

Macy nodded and then leaned her head against his chest. Her breathing had almost returned to normal. The muscles in her legs still ached, but the burning had at least stopped—for the time being, anyway.

It felt like ten minutes passed as they sat together in silence. It could have been just a couple minutes, but it was too hard to tell. Time had a way of passing at different speeds since she had been kidnapped.

Luke sat up straight, causing Macy to also. "I think we need to make a run for it now. Or perhaps a walk for it. Walking would be a lot quieter. We don't need to alert him to our location." He looked at Dorcas. "We already know he's out there. You should go home. That way you'll be safe and no one will be any wiser."

She shook her head. "I need to know that you guys are safe, Luke."

He let go of Macy and put a hand on Dorcas' shoulder. "Dorcas, you're dear to me like a sister. Please, go home. I need to know that you're safe too. We'll be all right. I promise."

Dorcas looked conflicted. "Whatever you say, Luke. I wish you both the best." She stood up and walked off.

He turned to Macy. "I had to say that line about her being like my sister. It was the only way she would actually go home. She has feelings for me that I can't reciprocate."

"Oh?" Macy didn't dare say more.

Luke lifted her hand and kissed the back of it. "Now to get you safely out of here." He pulled her up before she could respond to the kiss. He looked at her, this time his face was serious. "Like I said, we need to walk. Be careful not to brush against the stalks. They're too noisy, but at least they're a great way to hide."

Macy nodded. Still holding her hand, he started walking, but their arms brushed against the corn, so he let go. It was for the better anyway because it was too difficult for Macy to focus when her hand was in his. They made their way through the corn mostly avoiding the stalks. Every once in a while, one of them would accidentally brush against one.

It looked like the fence was visible in the distance. "Are we almost out of here?" Macy whispered.

"Pretty close, but don't get too confident."

"That's right, Heather." Chester jumped out in front of them.

Unable to contain herself, Macy let out a blood-curdling scream.

Luke spread his arms out, acting as a shield between Macy and Chester. He looked back at Macy. "Run."

"Not without you."

He gave her an exasperated look. "Go! I'll catch up."

Chester gave an evil laugh. "No, he won't."

"Don't listen to him. Run, Macy!"

"Her name is Heather." Chester shoved Luke.

"No. Her name is Macy. That's the name her real parents gave her, you lawless heathen."

"Heathen? Who are you calling a heathen? I'm about to be anointed as a high prophet. If you repent, I might consider granting you forgiveness for your trespass, young man."

"You're the last person to be able to give me absolution." Luke turned to Macy again. "Run, will you?"

"Sorry, I won't leave your side, Luke."

Chester grabbed Luke's shirt and choked him. "I'm not going to offer this again. Go now and save yourself. I may even consider going easy on

Heather if you run. Nobody else needs to know about this."

Macy smelled smoke. The fence must have finally been engulfed in flames. If they could just get away from Chester, they would be able to make their escape. "Luke, it's okay. Go. I don't want you getting hurt."

Chester pulled on Luke's collar again. "Listen to her. She knows what's good for you." He let go of Luke's shirt and shoved him back. "This is your last chance. Don't test me."

Luke fixed his collar. "Macy deserves to go back home to her family. You're not her family. Why do you need her? You and Rebekah can have your own kids."

Chester furrowed his eyebrows. "Not that it's any of your business, Son, but Heather is my daughter and I will not lose her again."

"You need to rethink that." Luke ran at Chester, ramming his shoulders into his chest. Chester gasped for air, stumbling back and looking surprised. He grabbed Luke's hair and shoved his face into a corn stalk.

Full of rage, Macy ran at Chester. She slammed into him, causing him to stumble slightly. Not even enough to let go of Luke. She dug her nails into his arm. He pushed his elbow out, but she wasn't going to let that stop her. She squeezed even harder. "Let go of him!"

"Macy, run! Get out of here," Luke begged.

"I wouldn't listen to him," Chester said. He let go of Luke and pried her off his arm. His eyes were full of anger, but she felt less intimidated with Luke at her side. The two of them could take him.

Luke jumped on Chester, knocking him down. Halfway through the air, Chester grabbed Macy's arm and pulled her down with him. Her face scraped along a stalk, burning as she went down. She landed with a thud and then rolled against Chester. Luke landed on his knees and punched Chester in the nose.

Chester shoved Macy off him and hit Luke in the jaw. Macy jumped up and grabbed his arm, trying to keep him from hitting Luke any more. Luke hit Chester in the cheek, barely missing his glasses.

Chester shoved Macy down. She stood back up and saw Chester and Luke were wrapped around each other, wrestling and punching on the dirt. She couldn't see a way to jump in without getting hit by either one of them.

She remembered the box of matches that Luke had given her. She pulled it out of her pocket and lit one. As soon as the flame came to life, she set it against the stalk of corn that had scratched her face. It took a moment, but it caught on fire, the flame simultaneously going up and down the stalk.

Macy put the match against another stalk and watched it light up as the match itself died. She looked over at Luke and Chester. They were on the ground, still fighting.

Chester's glasses gleamed in the light of the fire behind her. Now was her chance to break those big, ugly glasses. She went over and reached down, grabbing them off his face. He shouted something at her, but she wasn't listening.

Behind her, she could feel the heat from the growing fire. Not only that, but she could hear the crackling and whooshing sounds as it moved along. The smoke tickled her nose and throat.

Before dropping the glasses on the ground, Macy kicked Chester just because she could. Then she stomped on the glasses, breaking them. The frames bent and the lenses were both broken into several pieces. Rage built in her gut and she jumped up and down on them until they were unrecognizable.

Chester yelled something, but Macy was too focused on destroying the glasses even further. Once she and Luke got away, she would never have to worry about keeping Chester happy again. She stomped on what was left of the glasses one more time for good measure and then turned to him and yanked on what hair he had, pulling him away from Luke.

There was just enough space between them that Luke was able to get up. Chester looked around, patting the ground, obviously looking for his glasses. Macy ran over to Luke and grabbed his hand. "Let's get out of here."

"My leg is hurt. I'm not going to be able to run. You should run ahead of me."

"What? I'm not leaving you behind. Get up." She yanked his arm.

"I'm only going to slow you down."

"Who cares? We're leaving together."

"Even if we get out of the community, I'm never going to make it to the main road."

"Yes you will. Hurry up before he attacks again. If he doesn't get us, the fire will. We're going to be surrounded soon."

Luke sighed and then nodded. He took a step, limping. Pain covered his face.

Macy gasped. "What did he do to you? Lean on me."

He did, and they made their way down the narrow path with the raging fire chasing them on one side. It wouldn't be long before Chester was also chasing them. She knew that the lack of glasses would only slow him down, not stop him. The only thing that would stop him would be if she shoved him into the fire—and maybe that wouldn't even do it.

"Are you sure you want me slowing you down?"

"How could I not, Luke?"

"My real name—"

A shot rang through the air. Macy looked around, unable to tell where it came from. She knew it had be Chester, but where was he?

Corn nearby rustled and Dorcas appeared. "You guys have to leave now. He's got a gun. I found a place to escape near the feed stable. I told some of the kids who want to get out. They're already headed there. We have to go *now*."

"I thought you were going home," Luke said.

Dorcas shook her head. "Not a chance."

Luke shook his head. "I should have known. I think my leg is strong enough to run on."

"Are you sure?" Macy asked. "You were just limping a moment ago."

"It's not as bad as I thought." He took her hand. "Follow me."

Several more shots rang through the air, but that time, Macy could feel the breeze of a couple bullets. "Get down!" she shouted.

She threw herself to the ground, pulling Luke with her.

"Are you okay?" she asked.

He didn't respond, but she noticed his hand holding his arm.

Fear squeezed through Macy's entire body. She couldn't breathe or talk. When more shots were fired, she found her voice, but it didn't sound like her. "Are you okay?" she repeated, her voice several octaves higher than normal. Macy moved his hand and could easily see a dark red spot on his white shirt. A horrible sound escaped her throat.

Luke looked into her eyes. "I'll be fine." His voice sounded pained. "It only grazed me. Let's go."

Another shot sounded, this time louder.

Dorcas screamed, clutching her stomach. Macy saw a growing red spot on the middle of her clothes.

Luke ran to Dorcas and she fell into his arms. "You guys have to leave me here."

Tears filled Luke's eyes. "I won't, dear sister."

"You have to or this was all for nothing. Luke, you have to escape and get out of here."

"Not without you. I'll carry you."

Dorcas shook her head. "You need to escape." Her eyes closed.

"No!" Luke shook her. "Don't close your eyes. You can't give up—we have to get out of here."

Dorcas opened her eyes slowly, looking at Luke. "I *am* getting away. But it's going to have to be up to you to get yourself out."

"Please don't. You can't talk like this."

Dorcas closed her eyes and she went limp.

Luke shook his head, tears flying. He shook her again, but Dorcas didn't respond.

"Dorcas," he whispered. Her head turned and rested on his chest.

"We have to go," Macy said, reaching for his arm. "I'm sorry."

Luke nodded, wiping his tears. He set Dorcas on the ground with care. "I've got to get you out of here." He took her hand again, getting Dorcas' blood on Macy.

They rounded a corner and came face to face with Chester.

Reality

ALYSSA SAT UP in bed, gasping for air and drenched in sweat. Another nightmare. That one felt so real.

Chad sat up. "Are you okay, Lyss?"

She shook her head, clinging to the comforter. "I had a horrible dream."

He scooted closer to her. "Tell me about it."

"Macy—she," Alyssa's lips shook, "was trapped somewhere, screaming."

Chad pulled her into an embrace. "It was only a dream."

"It didn't *feel* like one." She was shaking. "It was so vivid."

"Your subconscious is working out your fears, that's all."

"There was a fire. I think she's in danger, Chad."

"Shh." He held her closer.

Alyssa pulled away. "I won't shush. I really think she's in trouble."

"I wasn't telling you to be quiet. I was helping to calm you, like when the kids were upset when they were younger." Though it was dark, he was pretty sure she glared at him. "What else did you see in the dream? Anything to identify where she was?"

"There was a blaze. She was outside. That's all I know. The longer I'm awake, the less I can remember."

"Do you want me to turn on the news and see if there are fires anywhere?"

"How would that help anything?"

"Let's say that somehow you two are communicating, it could help us find her. Think about it, Lyss. It's winter. There aren't likely many fires. It's not like in the summer, when there are a lot of wildfires. In the summertime, a dream like that wouldn't be helpful. But now, it could be."

"So you believe me?"

"Of course." Chad wasn't sure that he did, but he wanted her to know he was on her side. He helped her up and handed her a robe before putting on his. They went into the bonus room and he turned the TV on, scrolling for the news.

They sat there, watching the ticker at the bottom of the screen as the reporter talked about the stock market. There was nothing about any fires.

Alyssa frowned. "There goes that theory, and you probably think I'm an idiot, to boot."

"Not a chance. Just because it's not on there, doesn't mean it didn't happen. If it's a small fire in an obscure location, it might never make the news. You practically have to burn a house down while trying to kill a spider to get the media to pick it up." Chad pulled out his phone and opened the browser app to search for fires. "Nothing online either. Sorry, Lyss."

Alyssa frowned. "We should get back to bed. I'm sorry I woke you up and made you get out of bed."

He clicked the remote, turning the TV off. "Nothing to be sorry for."

When they settled back into bed, Alyssa turned to him. "Do you think we'll ever get her back? Or do you think that girl from Clear-view…?" Tears filled her eyes.

"No. I don't think it's her. There's no other evidence of her being there. All of her stuff has been found locally."

"I hope you're right. But they haven't found anything else in a while. It—"

"Get some sleep, Lyss. We both need it. The DNA results will be back soon enough. I'm sure they'll find that it's not Macy."

"But it's such a small town and there aren't any missing girls in Clear-view."

"Remember what Detective Fleshman said? There are a lot of missing girls, but most don't make the news. Girls who—"

"Know what? You're right. We should get some sleep. I don't want to think about this right now. No statistics. Sleep is what's going to help us.

That and positive thinking."

"That's right. Send her positive thoughts. Macy will get them." He kissed her forehead and held her until her breathing deepened. Then he rolled onto his own pillow, unable to get back to sleep.

It was so hard to know what to think. He wished that real life was more like those shows—instant DNA results. Why had their dentist office have to catch on fire? And why hadn't they kept their records online? It wasn't like it was the nineties or they were living in some third world country.

On one hand, he really just wanted answers. Then they could all move on with their lives, one way or another. Of course the last thing he wanted was for Macy to be dead, but at the same time he hated living in limbo. If she was gone, they deserved to know the truth. She wouldn't have wanted them living like this.

Tears filled his eyes. He hated thinking about what Macy would or wouldn't have wanted. It was the last thing he should have to think about. No parent should outlive their child. From the moment she was born, he felt like his heart lived on the outside of his body, running around. It was now split in two. One half here at home, safe and sound, and the other out there somewhere—hopefully still alive.

How had his life spun out of control so fast? He had been on the fast track to the career of his dreams with his blog picking up popularity so fast. Had he done something wrong? Was he to blame for any of this?

Was he being punished for spending too much time working, ignoring his family? He thought he had been working hard for them, so they could have a better life once it took off. The plan had been to be able to quit his job, and then he would have had all that extra time to spend with them.

It was clear now—too late—that he should have spent more time with them. He didn't know nearly enough about either of his children. That much had been made clear since Macy disappeared.

Or was he being punished for his relationship with Lydia? He had cut that off even though she kept turning up whenever he went out. Chad had done everything he could to make that right—short of fessing up, and that wasn't going to happen. He told Lydia it was over and he was working on his marriage. Alyssa loved him again and he her.

All they need was to have Macy back and everything would be as good as it had been years earlier when they'd had the dream life. He hadn't appreciated it then, and now he was paying for it. He looked up toward the ceiling and promised anyone or anything that might be listening that he would never take his family for granted again.

Dark

LUKE YANKED MACY'S arm, pulling her away from Chester. Her feet stumbled underneath her, but she managed to get her footing and keep up with Luke. He ran so fast it was hard for her to keep up, but the adrenaline helped. Luke hadn't been kidding about his leg being okay. Either that or it was adrenaline, like Macy felt. Whatever it was, hopefully it would serve to keep them alive.

She heard Chester chasing them, but it sounded like he was having a hard time without his glasses. It sounded like he kept running into the corn stalks.

"Is your leg going to be okay?" Macy asked.

"Yeah, but we need to hurry."

"How far away is the feed thing Dorcas mentioned?" Macy asked.

"Not too far, but it won't be long until someone discovers the opening and blocks it. That's why we have to hurry."

They darted between corn stalks, turning down new rows constantly. Finally, they broke free. Luke stopped for a moment and looked around. He pointed right. "This way."

They ran toward some buildings that reminded Macy of the barn back at Chester's parents' farm. Her throat closed up even as she ran. If Chester planned to lock her up again, she would fight him until the death.

Luke led her past those and down a little path. "The fence isn't far off. Hopefully the opening is close."

They passed the barn-like buildings, this time around the back. Macy saw something unusual in the fence about twenty feet away, but even though her eyes had adjusted to the dark, it was hard to tell. They were far enough from the fire they'd started that she couldn't even see any sign of that, either.

"I think I see it," Luke said. He led her to the spot Macy had seen.

When they got there, it was a small opening, barely big enough for one person. "You go first. You're so tall, I'm worried you might not fit," she said.

"All the more reason for you to go first." He let go of her hand and extended his arm toward the opening. "Go."

"I want to make sure you'll fit first."

His eyes narrowed. "Go!" he shouted, looking angry. "If I have trouble you can help pull me through."

Macy jumped and then ran to the spot and squeezed through, scratching her hand and face in the process. When she was fully out she looked back in. "Come on."

"Sorry to speak harshly. It was the only way I could get you to go first."

"I don't care. Go through."

Luke looked away. "People are coming."

"Hurry!" Macy put her arm through and grabbed his hand. "We've got to go."

He slid his fingers through hers and slid about halfway through the hole.

"What are you waiting for?"

"I'm stuck."

"Are you serious?" Macy exclaimed. She let go of his hand and pulled on the fence. The wood wouldn't budge. "Hold your stomach in or something." She pulled harder on the plank and her hand slipped, bending a nail all the way back. She let out a cry of pain.

Worry covered Luke's face and he pushed against the wood. It buckled under his grip. He fell to the ground next to her, nearly knocking Macy over. She moved out of the way and grabbed his hands, helping him up.

Voices could be heard from the other side of the fence.

Luke put a finger up to his mouth and pointed to the right. He slid his fingers through hers and squeezed.

Macy held her breath as they tip-toed away. She could make out

Jonah and Eve's voices yelling about the hole in the fence.

Luke and Macy continued walking quietly until the prophets' voices faded away.

He looked into Macy's eyes. "Now."

They both burst into a run.

"Listen for the others," Luke said. "I'm not sure who escaped, but we have a better chance at getting away with more people."

"What if we run into a prophet? Or someone else who wants to take us back?"

"We'll run from them obviously, but Dorcas said some of the kids got out. We have to find them."

Macy nodded and they ran in silence.

Something howled in the distance, sending chills down her spine. "Maybe we should just head for the highway."

Luke shook his head. "That's what they're going to expect. We need to go through the woods and find the world on the other side."

"Maybe." She didn't like the idea of going farther into the woods, but she wasn't going to leave Luke's side.

He squeezed her hand. "I'll keep you safe. I promise."

They ran in silence for a while and then Luke slowed down. "Do you hear that?"

Macy listened. All she heard were owls and the occasional coyote. She shook her head.

"I think I hear the others. This way."

They ran through the thick trees and bushes barely able to see. At least they were far enough away from the community that Macy couldn't hear the sounds of it any more.

"Where are the others?" Macy asked.

"Not far. Can you hear them now?"

"What am I supposed to listen for?"

"Conversation."

"I really don't know how you hear it."

"I used to stand guard at night for a while," Luke said. "I learned to listen for the smallest sounds."

Macy strained to hear something, but she couldn't hear anything beyond the running of their feet or the howling animals in the distance.

Luke slowed, forcing Macy to also. She could hear something—finally. She could barely hear hushed whispers. They crept toward the noise. There were some swishing noises and Macy found herself face to face with about half a dozen kids all wearing white. They were standing defensively, like they were ready to attack.

Macy held her breath. She didn't know how much more she could take.

One near the front relaxed. "It's just Luke and Heather."

The others changed their positions, each looking relieved.

"How did you get away?" asked the one in front. Macy couldn't remember his name. "The fire was all around the opening."

Luke pulled Macy close and wrapped his arm around her. "We found another way out. We were near the corn fields."

"Are they coming after us?"

"They're sure to," Luke said, "but for now, we appear to be in the clear."

"We need to set up camp somewhere."

"Do we have any supplies, David?" Luke asked. "I've got matches, but not much else."

David shook his head. "We weren't prepared to leave."

"Then we're better off moving," Luke said.

"Everyone's tired. We need to get some rest," David said.

Luke stood taller against Macy. "We're going to be a lot worse off than tired if the prophets find us. Who's with me?"

Most of the others behind David agreed with Luke.

"Good," said Luke. "The farther away we get, the better. Once we reach the world, we can speak with their authorities and get the help we need. For now, we just focus on getting there."

"Let's discuss a plan," David said.

"Yes, let's." Luke turned to Macy. "Sit down and rest. I'm not sure how long we're going go before we rest again."

"At least we're free. I can't believe I'm away from Chester." Macy looked around, never having felt more free.

Luke wrapped his arms around her and placed his lips on hers softly. "And I'll make sure you're not just away from him, but that you get back to your family."

What will happen to Macy next? Will she manage to get back to her family?

Find out in the final book in the trilogy: Over – *now available!*

Other books by Stacy Claflin

Gone series
Gone
Held
Over
Complete Trilogy
Dean's List (Standalone)

The Transformed Series
Deception (#1)
Betrayal (#2)
Forgotten (#3)
Silent Bite (#3.5)
Ascension (#4)
Duplicity (#5)
Sacrifice (#6)
Destroyed (#7)
Hidden Intentions (novel)
A Long Time Coming (Short Story)
Fallen (Novella)
Taken (Novella)

Seaside Hunters (Sweet Romance)
Seaside Surprises (Now Available)
Seaside Heartbeats (Coming Soon)
Seaside Dances (Coming Soon)
Seaside Kisses (Coming Soon)
Seaside Christmas (Coming Soon)

Other books
Chasing Mercy
Searching for Mercy

Visit StacyClaflin.com for details.

Sign up for new release updates.
http://stacyclaflin.com/newsletter/

Want to hang out and talk about books? Join My Book Hangout
facebook.com/groups/stacyclaflinbooks/

and participate in the discussions. There are also exclusive giveaways, sneak peeks and more. Sometimes the members offer opinions on book covers too. You never know what you'll find.

Author's Note

Thanks so much for reading Held. One thing I love about writing a series is the chance to get to know the characters better, watching them grow and change in new circumstances. In this trilogy, most of the characters become stronger due to the tragic circumstances in their life. I think that's true in real life, which is part of what makes the trilogy so intriguing. I think we all ask ourselves how we would react if we found ourselves in their shoes.

If you enjoyed this book, please consider leaving a review wherever you purchased it. Not only will your review help me to better understand what you like—so I can give you more of it!—but it will also help other readers find my work. Reviews can be short—just share your honest thoughts. That's it.

Want to know when I have a new release? Sign up here (stacy-claflin.com/newsletter/) for new release updates. You'll even get a free book!

I've spent many hours writing, re-writing, and editing this work. I even put together a team who helped with the editing process. As it is impossible to find every single error, if you find any, please contact me through my website and let me know. Then I can fix them for future editions.

Thank you for your support!
~Stacy

Made in the USA
Middletown, DE
14 January 2017